Quentin Mouron is a poet and a novelist. He was
born in Lausanne in 1989 and is Swiss and Canadian.
In 2012 he won the Prix Alpes-Jura for his novel *Au
point d'effusion des égouts.* He has written three other
highly acclaimed novels before *Three Drops of Blood
and a Cloud of Cocaine,* which is his first work to be
made available in English.

THREE DROPS
OF BLOOD AND A
CLOUD OF COCAINE

Quentin Mouron

Translated by W. Donald Wilson

BITTER LEMON PRESS
LONDON

BITTER LEMON PRESS
First published in the United Kingdom in 2017 by
Bitter Lemon Press, 47 Wilmington Square, London WC1X 0ET

www.bitterlemonpress.com

First published in French as *Trois gouttes de sang et un nuage de coke*
by Éditions de la Grande Ourse, Paris, 2015

The translation of this work was supported by the Swiss Arts Council Pro Helvetia

A CIP record for this book is available from the British Library

ISBN 978–1–908524–836
eBook ISBN: 978–1–908524–843

Typeset by Tetragon, London
Printed and bound by CPI Group (UK) Ltd, Croydon, CR0 4YY

Am I really capable of *that*? Is *it* even serious? Absolutely not! Not in the least! It's just my imagination playing a game, a fantasy for my own amusement. A game! Yes, that's what it is, a game!

DOSTOEVSKY
CRIME AND PUNISHMENT

When a person loses all hope and purpose, he can sometimes become a monster out of sheer boredom.

DOSTOEVSKY
NOTES FROM THE HOUSE OF THE DEAD

For my parents

FIRST DAY

1

The black pickup is standing at the corner of Parker and Mount Auburn. Old Jimmy Henderson has left the engine running and is consuming the last of the slice of pepperoni pizza bought from the eatery on the corner. The cabin smells of frying oil, fresh blood, and stale tobacco smoke. The floor is strewn with food wrappers and empty drink cartons. A piece of deer carcass wrapped in plastic is lying on the passenger seat. A hunting gun – a Winchester 12 pump-action shotgun – leans against the dash. A deodorizer depicting the crucifixion hangs from the rearview mirror.

Mount Auburn Street is quiet. The grocery store has just closed and night has fallen. In his rearview mirror Jimmy can see the First Baptist Church, now converted into mid-range apartments that are much coveted by neighborhood families. He once knew such a family, the Wallaces. The husband is dead now. He was tinkering with an old Corvette in a friend's garage when a clumsy slip of his screwdriver sent fuel spurting from the tank. He was smoking at the time, so he set off a huge explosion. His widow still mourns for him. The urn containing his ashes sits on the kitchen table. "We eat together every evening, just the two of us," she says. The First Baptist Church was built in the early twentieth century. Enormous, squat, and square, it has neither the austere charm of some small Boston churches nor the stiff majesty of the Church of the Holy Cross. This is the perfect setting for modest dramas – perfect for this person's drinking problem, for that one's gambling addiction, for infidelities – and perfect for old Mrs. Wallace weeping in front of her urn. For old Jim, outside in the street, it's an entertaining picture. Seen from inside, at the table, through the widow's eyes, everything has a different consistency. She can hardly be expected to find it amusing.

Jimmy turns on his headlights. He is about to drive off when he notices the figure of a man walking toward Mount Auburn from the end of Parker Street. He isn't the sort you expect to come across in Watertown: he is too impeccably dressed. People do dress up around here, of course. The big downtown families give cocktail parties to which tuxedos are worn – this isn't the boondocks, after all. But there's always something affected, forced, and ostentatious about the big shots who are invited. The man approaching is elegant. His dark overcoat is sober and perfectly cut, as are his trousers. He is wearing gloves. His shoes are patent leather. He comes closer. Jimmy can make out his face. About thirty. Good-looking. Dark hair. Clear eyes. Regular features. He comes up to the truck and stops.

"Good evening," stammers Jimmy. The man gives a slight bow.

2

Standing at the corner of Phillips Street and Mount Auburn, the Church of the Redemption is a bunker surmounted by a blinking neon cross. Around it is a metal railing to which a "For Sale" sign is attached. When Franck reaches the front of the church, three men are engaged in a lively conversation on the steps.

He clears his throat, and calls out, "Good evening."

The men jump.

"I'm sorry," says Franck, "I didn't mean to interrupt."

At first no one answers. A mustachioed fifty-year-old looks him over from beneath his lowered brow, while the other two, visibly uncomfortable, keep their eyes glued to the concrete.

The mustachioed man finally asks, "You're not from around here, are you?"

Franck smiles, graciously. "God hasn't granted me that good fortune."

"So where are you from, if you don't mind me asking?"

Franck thinks that the speaker resembles an actor whose name escapes him, in some series (the name of which also escapes him). But he is certain he's talking to a cop. "From New York."

"Don't tell me you came all the way from New York just to hear three miserable Clementi sonatas!"

"I came from Toronto, to be precise."

"I beg your pardon?"

"I live in New York, but I came here from Ontario."

"So you're just passing through?" asks the cop, his tone more abrupt than intended.

Franck, who has stopped smiling, looks him in the eye. "I'm here for a few days."

The cop turns away and looks at his watch. "It's time to go in."

"Do you mind if I ask your name?" says Franck.

"I'm sorry. I'm Paul."

Aged around fifty, with graying hair, Paul McCarthy has been sheriff for about a decade. He is one of the most respected figures in Watertown and an active member of the Church of the Redemption.

Inside, half the seats are occupied. The audience is made up of families and elderly folk. The concert is free. As they enter people are invited to make a donation to be shared between the pianist, the church, and a charity in aid of Haitian children. McCarthy takes out a twenty-dollar bill and slips it into the little metal cashbox. Franck does likewise. His entrance has been noticed. No one here dresses up to go out, or wears patent leather shoes. McCarthy turns to Franck: "Would you like to sit with us to hear the concert?"

"If you don't mind."

"My wife and daughters are sitting up front. Let's join them."

*

The McCarthys, followed by Franck, leave the church. Outside, snow is falling on the red brick buildings. The sheriff's cell phone rings and he moves away. Franck takes the opportunity to approach the pianist. "I've always considered Clementi a third-rate composer, but you were able to make him quite appealing."

"Thanks. He's not my cup of tea either, to tell you the truth."

"But maybe your bread and butter!"

"That's a hard thing to hear!"

"Not at all, I've very sharp ears!"

They laugh.

McCarthy goes past without seeing them, almost at a run.

"Paul, you're not staying?" asks the pianist.

"I have to go."

"There's an emergency?"

The sheriff stops and turns around. He sighs. "A murder."

Franck and the musician had indeed heard sirens a moment before. As they move toward the street they can make out the blue and red flashing lights further on, a few blocks away, at Parker Street.

"My God… it's rare for that to happen around here," murmurs the pianist.

"Well, it has to happen somewhere," Franck replies. Then he nods and brusquely holds out his hand to the pianist. "Very glad to have met you – sincerely."

3

By the time Sheriff McCarthy reaches Parker Street, the crime scene has already been secured. Two unmarked cars are parked on Mount Auburn. The sheriff's deputy, Gomez, is there, along with Jaspers and a third, younger man whose first name he has forgotten. McCarthy surveys the scene. The door of the pickup is open. A bloodstained white sheet covers the body.

"Jimmy Henderson. Lives in the neighborhood," begins Gomez.

"I know him."

Living just a few blocks apart, Paul McCarthy and old Jimmy used to bump into one another regularly in the 7-Eleven, at the car wash, at the service station, and, more recently, at a book club devoted to Western novels. They had never exchanged more than a few words, but they weren't total strangers. So the sheriff's voice trembles slightly as he asks, "Any idea what happened?"

Gomez lifts the top of the sheet. McCarthy is dumbfounded. He has seen dead bodies in Watertown before – the tragic residue of drunken brawls outside bars or nightclubs, victims of muggings committed by drug-starved addicts or illegals awaiting deportation; he has also had to deal with the settling of scores between motorcycle gangs;

he even saw the lifeless corpse of Tamerlan Tsarnaev, the Boston bomber, before the Feds took it away. Bodies with their throats cut like old Jimmy's aren't rare. Yet this is the first time he has been confronted with a corpse with the eyes slashed, the tongue cut out, and the cheeks gashed up to the ears.

"For God's sake!"

Mechanically, he registers the details. He lingers over old Jim's black pickup, a rust-eaten 1998 Ford F-250 with a dent in the left rear fender and paint chipping off in places. It is the kind of vehicle turned out by the thousand each day, anonymous, modestly customized by three bumper stickers: *Support Our Troops, Go Red Sox,* and – eliciting a sorrowful smile from McCarthy – *Born to be Free.* The sheriff looks in the back of the truck: wrapping for a fishing rod, a full gas can, an emergency triangle, and a padlocked metal box. He takes this out and shows it to Gomez.

"Have the keys turned up?"

Gomez pulls out a plastic bag. Attached to a key ring honoring the US Navy are three metal keys, in addition to a more substantial one for the pickup.

"One of these?"

"Find it for me."

The deputy pulls on a pair of vinyl gloves.

McCarthy turns to the body under the sheet. A pair of brown boots at least fifteen years old protrude from under it. The soles are worn. The jeans, with their hems too high on the leg, are also worn and patched. Probably bought in some supermarket.

Gomez opens the box: fishing line, weights, a Phillips screwdriver, an empty Marlboro cigarette package, Laramie cigarette papers, and an outdated advertising flyer for automobile accessories. Gomez next shows him the Winchester, and then the package of meat. Anticipating the sheriff's question, he says, "Venison, from the smell."

McCarthy nods. "Jimmy was a hunter."

Yes, Jimmy was a hunter. He was an ordinary guy; perfectly ordinary. In this country there must be millions of hunters in their seventies who drive a Ford truck, eat their pizza on the corner of an empty street, smoke Marlboros they leave in a box, support the armed forces, wear brand-name boots, and prefer to use cheap fishing line from Walmart rather than a Seaguar line that breaks just as easily. Millions! But, thinks McCarthy, those millions don't end up with their throats cut and their eyes sliced open.

4

Franck is walking in the night. It is snowing. This is his first time in Watertown, but he is familiar with the atmosphere of these eastern towns, sometimes poignant when the moonlight slants through a veil of falling snow, sometimes disturbing when a cry from an alleyway or nearby house shatters the nighttime silence.

As he is going along Palfrey Street, a panhandler emerges from a cross street. He stinks of alcohol and urine. His beard is tangled and filthy. Greasy hair sticks out from under the edges of his woolen hat and seems to spill over his face. He walks with a limp.

In a voice hoarse from years of poverty, excess, and exposure to the elements he asks, "Could you spare some change, mister?"

Franck stops. He doesn't answer. The panhandler grows bolder: "Mister… Please… I'm…"

"I know," Franck interrupts him curtly. "I know perfectly well what you're going to tell me."

"If you could—"

Franck slips his hand into his pocket. "How much do you want?"

"Five dollars, two dollars, even a buck! If you only knew… Let me explain, let me tell you my story—"

"It's not your story, buddy, it's the story they all tell. Do you know how you're going to end up? Murdered by some guy just like you, at a street corner just like this, on a night just like this. He'll have worked for Ford too, or GM, or Walmart; like you, he'll have begun to drink, then lost his job, and then his wife; he'll also have had to suffer the contemptuous looks of women he desired, and eventually have given up the very idea of sex. Like you he'll have seen his future and his past melt into a murky present. Like you he'll have become a shadow among the shadows in a town that can barely claim the name. I know that story well, my friend."

Franck stops speaking, and stands still. Eyes raised to the dark tops of the low buildings and the utility poles, he is reflecting: each time this guy asks somebody for money, maybe he gets something, maybe he's ignored, or maybe he gets a beating. A strange guy. Weightless, entirely without substance. Merely a shadow. If he's still alive, it's because it hasn't yet occurred to anyone to kill him. Would there be any more concern for his corpse than for a bag of garbage? Likely not. Anyone can slip him a coin, or slit his throat and – no, not slit his throat, let him go hang. That's it: his life hangs entirely on the whims of passersby.

Franck takes out a five-dollar bill. He throws it to the panhandler, who gazes at him open-mouthed.

"Now clear off!"

5

The Grand Conference Hotel, which stands in the heart of Watertown, has an absurdly magnificent air in comparison with the rest of the town. The massive art deco style building was erected in 1927, requiring the sacrifice of thirty or so traditional homes. The developers, banking on an imminent recovery of the economy (which since the end of the war had left the Boston region deep in the doldrums), wanted to make Watertown the natural destination for the business meetings of executives working in Boston (or "*for* Boston," as they liked to say). This ambition lasted for two years, with some measure of success, but then the Great Depression of 1929 forced the owners to sell off the huge building for a song, after which it remained empty until the early 1950s. When the city of Boston later became prosperous again, it became the breast at which the surrounding municipalities could suckle. The Watertown hoteliers did a roaring business until the mid-1970s. The recession, along with the various economic upheavals of the past forty years, put a damper on the Grand Conference Hotel's prosperity. But today it remains an establishment with an international reputation that is able to boast a substantial clientele.

Sitting at the hotel bar, Franck is sipping a glass of Nuits-Saint-Georges. Around him, businessmen are conversing in hushed tones or are absorbed in the screens of their tablets. A young woman – who might have been attractive if she didn't look so vacuous – is clinging to the arm of her admirer, a dapper guy of about fifty who, Franck surmises, is something of a rake thanks to Viagra and the occasional dose of laxative. This little world bathed in the subdued lighting of the hotel bar doesn't impress Franck any more than the world of the street – the world of addicts, beggars and welfare cases – or the world of ordinary Watertown folk consumed by their neuroses. These are not really worlds or universes, he reflects, setting down his glass, but more like those dolls that fit one inside the other. Sometimes, because of some irregularity, one of them has to be forced, smoothed down, or eased into place. Even so, the same interests always prevail together; only the way they do so is different... And yet... in a crime, the way you wipe your knife clean...

For Franck, any communication with individuals at the bar, even reduced to a minimum (in other words, usually a glance of understanding followed by a nod), is tiresome. If he does sometimes enjoy a chat, even on the most trivial of subjects, his inability to experience episodes of social existence on a primary level, to allow himself to go along with a set of conventions which deep down he calls "the comic illusion," doesn't allow him to derive any great pleasure from the barstool exchanges occasionally sanctioned by the intimate atmosphere of the Grand Hotel. If only these people weren't so fatuous, or were simply less credulous...

The receptionist is coming across the room toward him. "Sir, I've been asked to give you this." An envelope, which Franck slips into his pocket.

"Thank you. Is that all?"

"Your bags have been taken up to your room."

Franck nods. Calmly, he finishes his burgundy, asks for the drink to be added to his bill, and sets off toward the foyer.

Sheriff McCarthy rubs his hands to warm himself up. He and his men are questioning the inhabitants of the neighborhood. No one has seen anything. No one ever sees anything. The picture of old Jim, his neighbor of thirty years, comes back to him again and again. Why? For pity's sake, why? The sheriff is wondering about the wallet found in old Jim's jacket, his hunting rifle and ammunition, the truck with the keys in the ignition. Why hadn't the killer taken anything? It can't have been that he was in a hurry or that he panicked, as he stayed around long enough to mutilate the corpse. No, if he didn't steal anything it was because he didn't *need* to, because it didn't interest him. Well then, wonders McCarthy, what *does* interest you, you sonofabitch?

Franck enters suite 478. He turns on the light. His two bags have been placed at the foot of the bed. He sits on it, takes the letter from his pocket and begins to read, then sets light to it and throws it into the fireplace. He opens the first bag, from which he takes clothes that he puts away in a closet: a black jacket, a lilac one, pants, shirts, a pair of ankle boots, four neckties, a bow tie, two pairs of gloves, and a dressing gown. Then he draws the blinds, lifts the other smaller bag onto the bed, and checks its contents: ten packs of Davidoff cigarettes, several booklets of matches, his toiletries, his pink gold Jacot watch, his pen, a jotter, a travel chess set, a little leather-bound notepad, a copy of Joséphin Péladan's novel, *The Supreme Vice*, Paul Bourget's *Essays in Contemporary Psychology*, a biography of Shestov, a laptop, a switchblade, a butterfly knife, a silver coffee spoon, an envelope containing a half-ounce of cocaine, and a Steyr TMP machine pistol fitted with a silencer.

The snow has stopped falling. Watertown is covered with a light white powder beneath which minor dramas continue to play out. Outside, Sheriff McCarthy goes from door to door, from theater to theater. Nowhere is there any appearance of fury or savagery. These people commit only rational murders, justified by drunkenness or necessity and tempered by tears and regrets. They are simple folk, disturbed by life. In room 478 of the Grand Hotel, Franck smokes a cigarette as he reads the Péladan novel. He sees a world weighed down by habit, by a drab determinism comprised of dust and iron filings. Of blinkered people, good only for wielding hammers and battering their neighbors with them. I wish for some kind of convulsion, some discord in the turgid melody of mankind, he thinks. Slowly, he turns the pages. He inhales the cigarette smoke. Perhaps that will never happen.

SECOND DAY

6

Later, in a better-informed age, the word "destiny"
will probably take on a statistical meaning.

ROBERT MUSIL
THE MAN WITHOUT QUALITIES

Alexander Marshall was born in 1967 in a suburb of
Orlando. His mother, a follower of the hippie movement,
became pregnant during a psychedelic rock concert in a
Fort Lauderdale barn. A few years later she stabbed her
son, and then cut her wrists. According to the doctors, it
was a miracle that Alexander survived. Maybe he himself
would not have described as a "miracle" an outcome that
sent him from foster home to foster home, on each occasion becoming the object of a pious, morbid pity that
made the evangelical affections of his new protectors more
hateful to him than the attempted infanticide of which he
had been the victim. When he was fifteen, Alexander was
taken in by the McCain family. This sterling couple, both
teachers steeped in pedagogical theory and charitable
intentions, thought their example would be enough to
steer the turbulent adolescent back to what they called "a
decent way of life." The McCains were probably the last to

show him any love, or, more properly speaking, feelings. They got their reward when, two years later, Alexander left home after beating them up and stealing their car, TV, bottles of liquor, and some cash. They never reported the theft. Marshall then set off for New York, where he lived for ten years, surviving on the proceeds of petty thefts and small-scale dealing, mostly using the money to pay for the crack cocaine to which he had been addicted since he was eighteen. In 1996 he met Tracy at a concert in a Brooklyn warehouse. He fell for her right away. They had sex in the toilet, and then at her place. Two weeks later she told him he was the biggest loser she had ever known. In a fit of rage, he beat her up. A neighbor intervened, and Alexander planted his Opinel knife in the man's belly. He was arrested that evening. Throughout his trial he kept repeating that he didn't know what had come over him. He also kept saying how much he loved Tracy. The judge prescribed treatment in a detox clinic and then sentenced him to ten years for attempted homicide. Granted early release, he was freed in 2005. For two years he went straight, selling hot dogs on 13th Avenue. He then set out for Boston, where he learned to forge vehicle registrations. The economic crisis affected criminal activities as well as legal ones, and it became increasingly difficult to get hold of luxury automobiles. Alexander found it hard to get along, especially since he was back on drugs. In 2008 he had to take refuge in Canada for a few weeks to escape the vengeance of a Chechen gang. When the latter was broken up, Alexander resumed his activities in the area, choosing this time to operate in the suburbs, in the Bellams neighborhood.

He met Laura Henderson – old Jim's daughter – at a Dunkin' Donuts in Watertown. Initially they combined forces to push drugs, and then moved in together. It wasn't long before Alexander had his eye on Laura's daughter, Julia. He began walking in on her when she was in the shower, and caressing her buttocks when she passed by him. Once, unable to get an erection, he inserted a finger in her backside. She complained to her mother, who pretended to be scandalized. But her association with Alexander was just beginning and must have been too profitable for protecting a young girl from abuse – even her own daughter – to be a major imperative. Julia then confided in Jimmy, who headed over to his daughter's place and declared that this time something had to be done. He added that he considered Julia his last hope of making something worthwhile of his life. When Alexander came home Laura explained to him that her father had threatened to report him to the police. Right then he was too stoned to think, but she made him promise to sort things out with Jimmy and apologize to the girl. By this time Alexander was already the subject of an investigation for theft and receiving stolen vehicles.

It was because Alexander was suspected of the murder of Jimmy Henderson that Sheriff McCarthy's men, under Deputy Gomez, came to pick him up at dawn from his place on Faulker Street. He didn't resist. He knew that the cops had surrounded the house, that they were heavily armed, and that his small weapon, a .22 semiautomatic rifle, wouldn't be of much use. His goose was cooked. Gomez handcuffed him and dragged him outside, half naked, to a squad car. They didn't jeer at him, as often happens. Nor did they beat him. "This all looks real serious," Marshall said to himself as the car started off. Laura wasn't there. She had left town the evening before without saying where she was going.

In a padded interview room in the Watertown Police Department, Alexander is sitting across from McCarthy. Gomez is beside the sheriff.

"Let's go over it again: old Henderson was about to turn you in, his daughter vamoosed without leaving an address, you have a record as long as a trailer truck, and you have no credible alibi... Do you still deny killing Jimmy Henderson?"

Alexander is pale, dripping sweat, his eyes bulging. He has slept for only an hour and is suffering from withdrawal, which doesn't make it any easier to find himself sitting across from a cop accusing him of murder.

"No... I've never killed anybody, I—"

"You never killed anybody, but you did plant your knife in a guy's gut back in 1996."

"I didn't kill him."

"It was close, if I'm to believe the report made by my colleagues in New York."

"I didn't mean to, I lost control—"

"Just like when you found out that Jimmy Henderson was going to turn you in for sexual abuse of an underage girl, which, given your record, should fetch you, let's say three, four years?"

"No! No..."

"And was it also because you lost control that you sliced him up like that?"

Gomez places a photo of the dead man in front of Alexander. He turns away, retches, and throws up on the floor, spattering the deputy's boots.

"No, I swear, I swear… Please… Yesterday evening I—"

"I know. You said so already. You went for a walk. But you don't remember where—"

"I was—"

"Stoned. So you don't remember if you went to call in at the church, if you ate a bacon cheeseburger, bought a pair of jeans, or cut old Henderson's throat and then took it out on his dead body."

On a nod from his superior, Gomez makes Alexander stand up and leads him back to his cell.

The Bellams had once been a quiet neighborhood. But in 1956 a grandiose real estate project, jointly promoted by the speculators of Fargo Inc. and the municipal authorities, resulted in the destruction of some colonial-style houses so that they could be replaced by concrete blocks and affordable housing for the new, low-paid Boston workforce at a moment when the region was undergoing an unprecedented economic boom. The Bellams (Faulker Street, Crescent Street, Downard Street, and Bartolomeo Avenue) became one of those much-deplored bad neighborhoods where alcoholism, violence, and suicide grew like mushrooms on damp moss – mushrooms whose growth accelerated at the end of the 1960s when the drug trade (and at the same time the repression of drug use) underwent a significant expansion. Between 1980 and 1995, tourist guides advised their readers to steer clear of the neighborhood, and even the cops preferred to conduct large-scale sweeps rather than see their patrolmen fall like flies under a hail of bullets from the guns of small-time, junked-up hoodlums and the local mafia. In 1986, Jon Harvey, the Republican mayor of Boston, solemnly promised to "cut the criminal networks to shreds" and "clean up the Bellams from the trash that has been accumulating there for thirty years." In 1988 Harvey was arrested for associating with organized crime and misappropriating public funds. It wasn't until 1994, a year marked by record levels of crime, that the authorities truly confronted the situation. Though it is no longer as unsavory as it was during the 1980s, the neighborhood remains, together with the suburb of Dorchester, the city's most significant hotbed of crime, and still has a bad reputation. Furthermore, the 2007 economic crisis witnessed a resurgence of behaviors that had been considered past history – vicious, barbarous killings for the sake of a beer or a pack of cigarettes, adolescent girls prostituted by their own parents, and so on. The Bellams boasts just a single church, which is tiny and in ruins, so some Bostonians see that as the mark of Satan, saying it is a lack of religion that has led its inhabitants to the edge of the abyss. The politicians in office, as well as those who, like Sheriff McCarthy, had been attempting for several years to restore a semblance of order to these neighborhoods, offer other explanations... They know all about the contempt heaped on the workers who were brought in during the 1950s only to turn up on the unemployment rolls twenty or thirty years later. They know how few obstacles were put in the way of the criminal gangs and drug cartels when they moved in and put roots down there; they know how easy it was for people to neglect the Bellams file when, in the mid-1980s, it became one of the most dangerous neighborhoods in the Greater Boston area. It was there that Laura Henderson and Alexander Marshall found a fertile terrain in which their activities could prosper. There are hundreds of other Laura Hendersons, hundreds of other Alexander Marshalls, all living on the proceeds of petty theft, swindles, and dealing. Sometimes gangs settle accounts, and some guy is found lying riddled with bullets between two garbage cans, or a cop turns up in a pool of his own blood. Occasionally too, a father runs amok and murders his wife, his children, or a neighbor. All the same, thinks McCarthy, they don't mutilate the body of an old guy sitting in his truck right there in the street and then leave the scene without touching his gun or his wallet. It's hard to imagine they'd even leave as much as his dentures—

"Sheriff…"

McCarthy looks up at Gomez.

"What is it?"

"Marshall's lawyer is here."

"Okay, then."

In spite of everything, and in spite of the statistics, the Bellams neighborhood sees itself as a typical district in the suburbs. Its streets, which are busy mostly at rush hour, only become intimidating after dark. Its inhabitants set off at seven in the morning to take Route 1, or to catch a bus from one of the five stops that serve the neighborhood. They work until four. In the evening they dream of a different life, or come face to face with the life they lead. In all their dreams it differs from the reality – but isn't it that way for just about everyone? The worker sees himself as a foreman, the foreman as a boss, and the boss as a shareholder. They all dream of a wife more beautiful than the one they have. They all dream of having children less stupid and more grateful than the ones they have. Dissatisfaction with life has nothing to do with social class. Still, in the Bellams more often than elsewhere, dissatisfaction flirts with crime or self-destructive behavior. That makes it more obvious. It becomes entitled to its own statistics, as well as to a succession of politicians and clergy who preach about the ravages wrought by poverty and drugs. McCarthy thinks of the dramas he has seen played out under his eyes between Crescent and Downard Streets. He thinks of the family quarrels, the emaciated faces of the junkies, the vicious murders, and the settlings of scores. None of that is peculiar to the Bellams. It all happens in other places too. But it seems to McCarthy that in other places crime looks like an avoidable accident, while in the Bellams dramatic events have an inevitable, definitive appearance. When a murder victim is found in a well-to-do home in the center of Watertown, people are shocked, scandalized. But when a murder victim turns up in the Bellams, people just shrug. So Jimmy Henderson's murder will be on the front pages of the newspapers this morning, reflects McCarthy, but when they find out we've arrested a suspect in the Bellams no one is going to bother asking questions, and the buzz will die down; the only things left will be brief news reports for the crime buffs – who'll admit that after all there wasn't a lot that could be done. That is what frightens Sheriff McCarthy most: the idea that nothing can be done, that the die is cast.

Gomez has returned to the sheriff's office.

"The lawyer doesn't want to see me right now... He's just pointing out that he doesn't understand why his client is in the cells when he hasn't been charged with anything, and all the usual crap."

"I see... Just tell them that he had a loaded gun on his nightstand, which has been illegal since 1996."

Gomez is about to leave the office when he turns around.

"Sheriff..."

"Yes?"

"Do you think Marshall was really the killer?"

McCarthy reflects for a moment.

"One thing I'm sure of is that he's the ideal culprit."

7

Joséphin Péladan was born in Lyon in 1858. His first job
was in a bank. He felt that this experience was, if not exactly
torture, at least trying enough to create in him a feeling
of disgust with the drabness of office life. His coworkers
were, according to him, dour-looking and impossible
to suspect of the slightest passion, except perhaps for
a marked interest in the stock market, while their wives
were tempted by "fashion" – the tastes shared toward the
end of the century by almost everyone with more income
than a laundry worker. On an impulse – one of those urges
that would later make people say of him that he was an
"eccentric" or a "visionary" – he set off for Italy. There,
among the Renaissance masters, he forged his tastes,
and especially his distastes. On his return to France he
combated materialism and devoted himself to mysticism.
Along these lines, all sound and fury, he founded the
Kabbalistic Order of the Rose-Cross, and later the Order
of the Catholic Rose-Cross, the Temple, and the Grail. He
had people address him as "Sâr Merodak" and was considered a brilliant author – though somewhat "flowery,"
and half-demented. In addition to an impressive amount
of art criticism, he wrote several essays, tried his hand at
the theater, and, above all, threw himself into a venture as

remarkable as it is forgotten: writing the seventeen volumes of *Latin Decadence*. His life, like his work, is characterized throughout by its anti-conformism, for in the late nineteenth century – like nowadays, in the early twenty-first century – sameness, born as much from materialism as from democracy, was the enemy that had to be overcome.

"*There is a sin of the flesh unknown to novelists, one that might be thought lost if it were possible for mankind to lose a vice. None accuse themselves of it in the confessional, and its name – demoniality – is not to be found in many dictionaries. It is the literary, patrician, decadent sin* par excellence *[…]: it consists in copulating with demons – men with succubi and women with incubi.*"

Franck lays the first volume of *Latin Decadence* on the nightstand alongside his pen and notebook. Suite 478 of the Grand Conference Hotel is filled with sunlight; the morning is glorious. Franck is wearing his purple dressing gown. He gets up. From the window he has a view across the hotel's parking lot to the Denny's restaurant, which offers all-you-can-eat pancakes from 4:00 a.m. until midnight, the disused water tower which serves as a billboard for Lanzmann Escrow & Co., the three buildings of the Super 8 Motel that faces the street, and the skyline provided by the near and distant blocks – a conglomeration of brick homes, small apartment buildings, supermarkets, service stations, and warehouses – streets and avenues where hundreds of thousands of individuals live, love, suffer, and die. He extracts a cigarette from his packet of Davidoffs, licks it up and down, and rolls it in the little pile of coke on the desk. The cigarette crackles and the room fills with a smell resembling turpentine and ammonia. Franck lies down on the bed and resumes his reading. "*The Middle Ages were poetic: in their fond naivety they were so eager to preserve the dignity of the human species that, unwilling to believe that evil could be the work of man, they made it the work of the devil and, rebelling against the idea that humans might be evil in the same way as they are good, they declared that the wicked were possessed and saw demons where there were only vices. By restoring to human devilry what had been ascribed to the Devil, demoniality is a creation of the flesh that consists in exciting the imagination by fixing one's desire on a dead, absent, or inexistent being.*"

Someone knocks on the door.

Franck hides the pile of coke in the desk drawer, runs a comb through his hair, and peers through the peephole. It is the maid, come to do the room. He opens the door.

"Sir… I'm sorry for disturbing you… I thought you were out."

Franck gives a tense smile. "In an hour I will be."

Sitting at the hotel bar, he is sipping an indifferent black tea and reading the local newspaper. The first page is devoted to the barbarous murder of an elderly Watertown man, Jimmy Henderson, as he sat behind the wheel of his pickup on the corner of Parker and Mount Auburn Streets.

"It's dreadful, isn't it?"

Franck looks up. The waiter. An African-American aged about forty, whose impressive stature, scars, broken nose, and missing tooth suggest that he must have been involved in quite a few brawls (unless, of course, he had played football). His badge introduces him as Carl.

"Maybe so," answers Franck, taking a sip of tea.

"There are really some sick folks out there, don't you think?"

Franck remains silent for a moment. "Maybe that guy isn't as sick as you might think," he finally answers.

"All the same, he disfigured the guy!"

"That's not important."

"Pardon?"

"What I mean is, it's just secondary. Basically, the guy just wanted to have a bit of fun. Maybe there's harm in that, but he's not the only one! Look around you: one guy goes bowling, another goes to a whorehouse, a third swallows an ecstasy pill… They all want to enjoy themselves, have a new experience—"

"But he killed a guy!"

"Well, some kinds of entertainment are more unusual than others, the way some people have a liking for spicier things."

"He sliced up his face…"

"That's just an embellishment, a refinement, which anyway, for me, diminishes the purity of the act from an aesthetic point of view, the way the effect of a masterpiece can be diminished by a frame that's too heavy, or lighting that's too bright."

The incredulous waiter looks at Franck. Does he really believe what he's saying? Is he just trying to be provocative? Carl doesn't know what to make of it. He'd like to question this guest, but he's already allowed himself to be drawn far enough beyond the bounds of the reserve demanded by his employment. Getting into an argument could earn him a reprimand, or even get him fired. In the Grand Conference Hotel you have to be careful when dealing with guests' indiscretions. On one occasion he had reacted when a bejeweled, crazy old woman kept him standing there for twenty minutes as she spouted such virulent racism that he didn't know whether to laugh or drag her to the deep freeze and leave her there for an hour or two to cool off. He had restricted himself to expressing his disagreement quite simply and in a tone that he tried to make as calm, gentle, and neutral as possible, given the circumstances. As a result, he was hauled up on the carpet by his supervisor who, as he sipped his Coca-Cola, told him that while he didn't agree with the offensive words of the crazy old woman, and he understood why the waiter had spoken up, what he had done was entirely natural and anyone else would have done the same, *as long as they were off duty.*

But if I'd been off duty, Carl thought, I'd have slaughtered her.

The outcome of this interview was a warning and an assurance that if it happened again the waiter would no longer be able to count on the Grand Hotel to continue paying his four kids' school fees.

Franck leafs through the newspaper. For the waiter's benefit he adds, "Anyway, there's a lot more in the paper than this murder." He turns the pages. "Let's see: two corrupt cops awaiting sentencing, a woman knocked down on a crosswalk, the Sox losing a ball game, a pair of African musicians arousing the enthusiasm of the crowd at God knows what festival, several upcoming charitable events, with citizens being strongly urged to get involved, and various associations looking for volunteers... And you can donate blood! And then there are still the vehicles for sale, the boats, the apartment buildings, and a long list of death notices. No cause for rejoicing there, and nothing very surprising. Now, take this murder: you find it bizarre. Well, you're welcome to think what you like, but you have to admit it's a success: it strikes a jarring note in the silence, and that's something."

The waiter restricts himself to a nod, and asks if he can be of any further service to Franck.

"Yes! Lend me your ears, let me explain my thinking! Things aren't boring in themselves, you see, it's just that they wear out. Something that has kept you amused for a while eventually becomes tiresome. Do you like women? By the time you get through twenty of them, you've had enough. You take drugs? How many ecstasy pills can you take before they make you sick? Books? There are very few worth rereading – less than a dozen; the authors and their works become like the most ordinary red sky, the most ordinary magnificent view: in time they become colorless, you tire of them. So for someone who's tired, who's 'browned off,' if I can use the term, murder can be an option. Maybe that's what it costs to *feel* something? A caprice just acts as a counter to boredom, and, just like it, it's neither good nor bad."

He must be an addict, or an artist – or maybe both. Carl has encountered quite a few of these characters who affect eccentricity and get together in a duplex on Main Street to smoke a few joints or blow a few lines of coke as they expound ludicrous theories about the essence of Art or the Nature of the Good, ideas they've forgotten by next morning when they're on their knees in front of the toilet, puking. Unless he's a fence for stolen antiques, or something like that, he adds to himself.

41

8

Franck makes his way to the hotel's underground parking garage and gets into his car, a black rented Chrysler 300C. He moves off, connects his hands-free, and calls his New York office. After three rings, his secretary answers.

"Franck! I was beginning to worry." She seems glad to hear his voice.

"Hi, Mariella. Much going on at your end?"

He leaves the underground garage and emerges onto Conference Street.

"Well, Cavendish is sure he's about to find little Lucy. Apparently she's been living with her father somewhere between Nebraska and Wyoming. Lefèvre caught three adulterers in the act, and one of the guys clocked him."

"What else?"

"Newman has just gone off on vacation—"

"That's what he's best at."

"But first he completed a successful surveillance of the Storm Rifle warehouses. He found out that the intruders were none other than the boss's son and his buddies, who were helping themselves to the merchandise and reselling it."

"Great. And Bergson?"

Franck turns right onto Paley Street.

"He's still taking care of the CEO of BIDH. He's got three weeks left in the job."

"Anything else?"

"No, you're the only one left, Franck!"

"I've just carried out a rather delicate contract."

"And you can't tell me what it was, right?"

"Right on, Mariella."

"And when will you get back?"

"I've no idea yet... In a few days, most likely."

He reaches Mount Auburn Street.

"Complications?"

Franck hesitates for a few moments. Finally, he answers, "No."

He passes Cimeo and Parker Streets, catching a glimpse of the Watertown First Baptist Church, now converted into condos.

"Do you want me to send you the list of our upcoming commitments?"

Parker is closed to traffic and the crime scene guys seem to be at work. In 80 percent of cases they find nothing useful, Franck thinks, and then replies, "No, there's no point, thanks. Let Cavendish, Lefèvre, and Bergson share the load of adulteries, suspicions, shady business, and paranoia."

Mariella laughs. "I suppose I should tell them so in those exact words!"

Franck also laughs. "No, no. Tell them the work they're doing is fantastic, essential, and varied. Explain to them that every marital infidelity is different, that every trashcan they turn out to vet its contents has a story, or even better, a personality."

*

Sherlock Investigations was founded by Franck in the late 1990s. Initially, it was a one-man operation, leaving him to sort through the contents of garbage bins in search of useful evidence, to shadow accountants on their visits to prostitutes, and to act as security for paranoid small bosses with smelly feet and armpits. Franck thought he had learned about humanity from novels, but during these years he rediscovered it in the sewer. Nauseated by the degrading work, which nevertheless brought him substantial profits and at which he excelled, Franck hired Bergson, a Jewish former librarian with a passion for crime novels. This allowed him, as a first step, to offload the marital cases, which he just couldn't take anymore. Bergson, whom he had at first found somewhat unpredictable, not to say capricious, was soon obtaining excellent results. Franck rented an office in the very heart of Brooklyn, and five years after setting up his company he was enjoying an outstanding reputation. Then he hired Newman and Cavendish, two sinister-looking but intelligent former cops. The first had resigned after an inquiry was opened into police violence, and the second had been fired for using narcotics while on duty. Older veterans, they soon got on well with Bergson. Next, Franck needed a secretary, and along came Mariella, a twenty-three-year-old Latino girl. Then Lefèvre, a French expatriate and former teacher who had had the good sense to resign from his post as he had been working up to a sexual assault on one of his students. Won over both by his vice and the way he controlled it, Franck had hired him after dragging the story out of him. After that, Sherlock Investigations never looked back. The team met with well-heeled clients in new premises on Madison Avenue. As for Franck, he rarely takes on an assignment himself. Adulterous affairs, surveillances, stakeouts, digital security, or acting as bodyguard don't interest him. His employees do exemplary work. His role has been reduced to supervising and coordinating them. In other words, he has nothing to do. Occasionally, however, he will accept what he calls a "special mission."

9

Deputy Gomez goes to fetch Alexander Marshall from isolation cell 1B and bring him to 2E, a long, narrow room that already contains three individuals. This isn't the first time Alexander has found himself in a police station in the state of Massachusetts. He knows how things work. He knows they'd never put someone seriously suspected of being a psychopathic killer in with a couple of hookers barely of age and a drunk no longer able to sit upright. The effects of withdrawal are still being felt, he is still feeling nauseous, but all the same, cell 2E offers him a little comfort, a kind of perspective.

"Does this mean I'm not suspected of murder?"

"No, it means we still can't prove you did it, but give us time—"

"Then why are you keeping me in?"

"You were arrested for possession of a loaded firearm—"

"Small caliber!—"

"You were as high as a kite, and we found a load of crack in your apartment. And add to that about fifteen vehicle registrations not in your name—"

"What does that prove?"

"—and suspected sexual harassment of a female minor."

"She never reported it!"

"Sorry, pal, Julia Henderson just left the station a moment ago. Even if you didn't kill the old guy, you'll be inside for a stretch."

Alexander Marshall isn't surprised. He should have expected it. Basically, he has nothing against crime or injustice. They have been his lot since birth, and he has become acclimatized to them. When he makes someone suffer, when he beats them, robs them, or allows them to undergo the torments of withdrawal before offering them a tiny packet at an exorbitant price, he knows he's committing what is usually called an injustice. For him, it is neither moral nor immoral. There is nothing immoral about animals copulating freely and openly, when the humor takes them. Transposed onto human society it becomes a moral question, but in nature it's an insignificant phenomenon. Himself the product of a mistake and a bungled murder, Alexander Marshall doesn't exactly live on the same plane as other mortals, and has never felt himself to be a member of society – "I fell by the wayside," he sometimes says. He leads an ordinary life made up of petty pleasures, occasional highs, and modest gratifications, like when he has sex with Laura Henderson or sits in a muscle car. Nor is there anything original or revolutionary about his thinking: there are the rich and the poor, and the poor have to take the money of the rich to become as wealthy as they – such is the essence of his system. On the other hand, his actions are much less costly for him than for others, as if he occupied a space within which the laws of gravity were more elastic.

*

It is 12:45 p.m. Gomez is last to enter the conference room, and takes his place alongside the sheriff. Sitting in a semicircle in front of them are officers Jaspers and Hendrix, Doctor Olson, and also Sergeant Wilde, from the Criminal Division. McCarthy takes a moment to study each of them. He has confidence in Hendrix, who has served under him for the past ten years. In Jaspers too, even if his violent excesses have sometimes resulted in unfavorable reports, reviews, and threats. Gomez has been clean for three years now, and is an excellent deputy. Doctor Olson is an honest practitioner, without any special talent; he hasn't yet solved his drinking problem, to judge by the bags under his eyes – and there's every likelihood that he went on a binge last night. As for Sergeant Wilde, he's the kind of irritating up-and-comer, as stupid as he is intransigent, able to solve a case but not to understand its underlying causes. The product of a radical Protestant culture and too many video games, Wilde is your typical nasty cop. But McCarthy is wary of him for another reason, for, since the murder took place within the municipality, on his territory, he doesn't understand why he has been saddled with a representative of the State Police.

Wilde seems to have deciphered McCarthy's resentful glare. "I know this is your investigation, Sheriff. But it does seem to have some similarities with the Sherman Valley case. Do you remember it?"

McCarthy nods. He does remember it, and he is furious. That was in 2001, he thinks. Where were you in 2001, Wilde? Huh? Sitting in front of your computer screen? Hiding behind your mother's skirts? In your bed fantasizing about all the girls that wouldn't give you a second look?

At the time, McCarthy had followed the investigation as an onlooker, in the media and from what colleagues in other departments told him. A young mother living in the Bellams had been found dead in the woods at Sherman Valley, a nature preserve close to Boston. Her eyes had been sliced and she had been liberally mutilated with a box-cutter. Suspicion fell on her former boyfriend, a violent alcoholic who had never recovered from their breakup. He had been released for lack of proof.

Gomez intervenes. "Do you really think the two cases are connected? If I remember rightly, the young woman in the Sherman case was savagely beaten and her aggressor assailed her dead body furiously before leaving the scene. In this case there doesn't seem to have been any outpouring of violence."

Doctor Olson confirms this. "That's right. Henderson's throat was cut from left to right, probably with a hunting or kitchen knife, then cruciform incisions were made in the eyes and on each of the cheeks with a finer blade – a small knife or a scalpel."

"Wait!" Gomez interrupts him. "You're saying that two weapons were involved?"

"Yes, that's my provisional conclusion."

"So there were most likely two killers…" Gomez continues his deduction. "The first killed Henderson, then the other took it out on the body…"

"That's one possibility," the doctor concedes.

"Or there could have been a single killer, using two weapons."

"Have you ever come across such a thing?" McCarthy interjects.

"Unless he returned to the scene. Maybe he wasn't sure Henderson was dead, or he began to feel he hadn't done enough—"

"That's just crazy," Wilde declares abruptly.

McCarthy gives him a withering look. "Sergeant, what I find just crazy is mutilating the body of a senior citizen out on the street of a family neighborhood. Don't you?"

Wilde doesn't answer.

McCarthy continues. "Let me point out a few more things. The killer or killers didn't think it necessary to dispose of the body deep inside a forest, the victim isn't a young woman, and there are hundreds of other unsolved murders that would benefit from the attention of a talented officer like yourself…"

Wilde is aware that nobody in the room likes him. All the officers, and even Doctor Olson, are either from the Bellams or Dorchester. They have known one another for years, they have all experienced difficult family situations, they all attended public schools. Some have not quite come through in one piece (he glances at Olson, who hasn't been able to conceal his hangover, and at Jaspers, whose superiors do their best to cover up his overzealousness). Wilde himself comes from central Boston and his father is a judge. They eat a healthy diet, drink in moderation, and play golf. Sometimes, it's true, Wilde's father allows himself an escapade outside the office to bed a young illegal immigrant, just as the son occasionally takes advantage of his privileges as a cop to beat down the price of a blow job performed in his police car by a street hooker, but such things aren't really of any consequence.

"Listen, if you object to my being here, why don't you discuss it with the DA?"

Another dark look from the sheriff.

"I'm following this case as an observer," Wilde continues. "If it turns out there's a connection with the Sherman Valley murder, we'll reopen the file. That's all. We don't have to appreciate one another." (You're right there, thinks McCarthy.) "But I'm asking you to be completely transparent, in line with the orders we've been given."

"Right," McCarthy goes on, knowing that there's nothing he can do about the DA's decision, "let's get back to business and recap: yesterday evening, probably between 5:30 and 6:00 p.m." (he glances at Olson, who confirms with a nod) "at the corner of Parker Street and Mount Auburn, one or more individuals assaulted Jimmy Henderson as he was sitting in his vehicle."

"Forgive me," Wilde interrupts, "but how can we be certain that he was in his vehicle?"

McCarthy pretends not to have heard. "The aggressor or aggressors cut Henderson's throat and then disfigured him." Anticipating Wilde's next question, he adds, "If he had been mutilated before being killed, the incisions would not have been as clean. The body had to be immobile, and Jimmy unable to defend himself. What's more, no one heard him cry out."

Wilde nods.

"We have a suspect," adds Gomez. "Alexander Marshall. A record as long as my arm and a conviction for attempted murder. Jimmy Henderson was going to throw him out for sexual harassment of his granddaughter, which provides a reasonable motive. His alibi is far from convincing as well: he says he was wandering about the town high on drugs – he no longer remembers where he went, nor when he came home."

"Have you any proof?" asks Wilde.

McCarthy stares at him. "I find you're strangely talkative for an observer, Sergeant."

"I'm just doing my job, Sheriff. So it looks as if you've no evidence."

"A thorough search of the home and Marshall's vehicle should teach us more. His stepdaughter's complaint allowed us to obtain a warrant."

"But this search hasn't been carried out yet... So you don't think he's guilty; isn't that it?"

McCarthy lets out a sigh. "This time you've scored a point. I can imagine Alexander Marshall killing a man in cold blood. There's no doubt he's capable of it. But it seems to me there's no way a guy like him would stick around to amuse himself with the victim's face, or leave without picking up Jimmy's wallet and gun – never mind the truck, for we mustn't forget the guy was a car thief—"

"Maybe he was afraid of compromising himself by selling a murdered man's vehicle?"

"Yes, but that doesn't explain why he didn't take the $150 that was in the wallet."

"So you intend to release him?"

"No, there are other charges against him. In addition, we still have to question Laura Henderson, Jimmy's daughter."

"Where is she?"

"I've no idea. Marshall says he doesn't know either. He told us that every three months or so Laura tends to take off without a word to anybody."

Gomez adds, "Her daughter confirms that. Laura Henderson goes off the rails now and again; she's filled with disgust for herself, for everyone close to her, for the life she's leading. In short it's the big spring clean: she sets off to recharge her batteries, change direction, get back into harmony, and all that bullshit."

Wilde intervenes again. "Okay, Sheriff. Honestly, we haven't really gotten anywhere, right? I'm not saying that to piss you off, but we have to face the facts: if it's not Marshall, it could be just about anyone."

Olson's pager goes off. He mutters an excuse and leaves the room.

"It can't be just about anyone, Wilde. Among the people who can really kill in cold blood – and they're not that numerous, take it from my experience – very few do it without a reason."

"So I suppose you're going to make inquiries with the psychiatric services?"

"That's my business. I just want to point out one thing: slowly mutilating someone you've just killed doesn't happen every day. Somewhere out there there's a guy who's not like anyone else. A crazy guy, in other words. And it's that crazy guy we have to find."

"So you're looking for a raving lunatic, is that it?"

"Ye-e-s," answers the sheriff, unconvinced by his own reasoning. "Except that you know, Wilde, lunatics don't necessarily go around on pink bikes dressed up as Mickey Mouse and with eyes the size of golf balls. They can be more… discreet."

Olson returns.

"Something new, Doctor?"

Olson is paler than before. McCarthy thinks that he must have gone outside to throw up.

"Since Jimmy Henderson's severed tongue wasn't found anywhere close to his vehicle, we thought it must be down his throat."

"And?"

"It's not there, Paul."

"Meaning?"

Olson hesitates. He looks at the sheriff. Then at Wilde. Then at the sheriff again. "That the murderer most likely took it with him."

10

Lance Le Carré's mansion was born of the union of a rapid fortune and an ostentatious taste for the neo-baroque. Built according to plans by Garnier and Weissbach as adapted by Paul Hunter, a well-known architect who worked for Walt Disney, the result is an enormous, tacky carbuncle as aggressive as it is heavy-handed, but one which secures its owner's reputation as an aesthete. Concerned about remaining faithful to his image, Le Carré devotes himself to the promotion of the arts and of artists – in addition to a considerable number of questionable activities in partner-ship with various Boston gangs. He can frequently be heard going on about some singer to whom he is "giving a head start," some "fiendishly promising" young visual artist, or some aged poet who has lost his sight because of illness and whom he is proud to support. His wife, Evia (not her real name), occasionally organizes fundraisers and charity soirées to provide assistance to the most poverty-stricken artists (she acts with a mixture of good intentions and gullibility, which has earned her the nickname "Sugar Mommy" among the Bostonian upper crust). The Boston Museum of Modern Art is indebted to them for significant donations, while the curator of the Watertown Museum of Armenian Art repeats to anyone prepared to listen (his nascent senility has something to do with this) that nothing would have been possible without these exemplary patrons of the arts. The mayor and councillors regularly sing their praises during council meetings. Their company is much sought after. The husband, short and stocky, the wife, slender and tall, stand side by side, sculpted in marble, at the end of an avenue of cypress trees by the entrance to their property, as if to welcome their visitors: artists, of course, but also producers, financiers, models, intellectuals, and judges. As for the underworld, it is requested to use the back door.

Franck parks the black 300C in a public lot adjoining the property. A surveillance camera tells him that his arrival has not gone unnoticed. Less than a minute later a side door opens and one of Le Carré's employees, a generously scarred hulk who Franck senses is armed, gestures to him to come in. Side by side, without exchanging a word, they climb a service staircase leading to the second floor, where a second hulk similar to the first meets them and begins a thorough body search to which Franck merely submits with a sigh. Then they set off again, and after a series of empty white corridors hung with chandeliers intended to cast light on some indifferent paintings, they reach a heavy oaken door. They knock. A voice tells them to enter.

Moist-lipped, with nasty eyes, Lance Le Carré is sitting behind his desk. He measures Franck up before greeting him. The detective, slightly nauseated by what he sees all around him (cheap copies of Renaissance masters in heavy wooden frames, bookshelves full of volumes with matching bindings that look as if they have never been opened, and knickknacks of no particular age or origin, acquired in bulk from unscrupulous antique dealers), responds with a nod.

Without a word, Franck steps forward. He puts a hand in one of his pockets and takes out a USB key, which he lays on the desk. Then, on a gesture from Le Carré, he sits down.

"First of all, let me congratulate you, my friend. This was a tricky business, but you were able to carry it off successfully."

"I carry off all my assignments successfully, Mr. Le Carré," replies Franck in a perfectly blank voice.

Le Carré suddenly seems mollified. "Are you sure no one saw anything?"

"Absolutely certain."

The man who had escorted Franck enters the room. He lays a black attaché case on the table and opens it. It is full of banknotes.

"All cash, and untraceable. You can count it."

"No need," Franck answers. He gets up, takes the attaché case, and holds out a hand to Le Carré.

"You're leaving? Didn't you get my invitation?"

"I did indeed, but our contract has now been fulfilled. So I'll go out the way I came in and then re-enter by the front door, as the guest of Evia and Lance Le Carré."

The businessman smiles, and shakes Franck's hand.

A youthful pianist is expending enormous energy on a Bach fugue that falls on deaf ears. The lighting is harsh.

The guests are chatting loudly; several masterpieces are on display for their admiration. In the main room, Evia Le Carré takes Franck on a round of the guests; for him it becomes a series of inane, painful stops. First comes Judge Malcolm, who almost reached the federal level; he had sincerely battled crime all his life until a bout of depression tinged with alcoholism left him at the mercy of the city's criminal gangs. He is tall, bald, slightly unsteady on his feet, with a serious, constantly preoccupied air. They pay their respects to the von Wirts, a pair of bankers who were very successful until the 2008 crisis but are now reduced to traipsing from drawing room to drawing room, grousing, mudslinging, and repeating wherever they go that they would rather be somewhere else. Then, from a corridor, there emerges an African-American Dominican monk wearing a white woolen scapular. He is Jack Loewy III, celebrated for his extravagance, his austere morals, and his participation in numerous charitable works. He has no idea that Lance Le Carré is a big shot in organized crime. Indeed, most of the guests are blissfully unaware of this. This bunch of well-heeled nitwits, thinks Franck, that some fanatics, for the most virtuous of motives, would like to see cast into the flames, actually seem quite decent, respectable, and soft-hearted. So, into the fire with them? By all means! But out of boredom, on a whim, for pure entertainment! As for morals, those shop-window smashers, cop haters, and throwers of Molotov cocktails aren't much more savory. Anyway, nothing seems very savory when viewed from a moral angle. Everything just turns black. It's a total eclipse.

Next, Evia and Franck greet Professor Caron, a physicist specializing in quantum theory, whose red hair and thick-rimmed glasses allow a glimpse of a childhood on which mockery and bullying have left their mark. Franck recognizes him: yesterday afternoon he saw him in the town, and had the definite impression that the man was following him. What's more, he has read his file: a cousin of Lance Le Carré's, a loner, a bit peculiar, who has been forced into early retirement for some unstated reason. Caron blushes as they shake hands. "I'm truly delighted to meet you; I've heard a lot about you, delighted!" Franck wonders how and why he can have heard of him. But Evia leads him away from the redhead, who, left standing by himself, continues to express his delight. "He's a relative of my husband's," she explains to Franck, who already knew this and has had time to picture him as a hanger-on, a parasite, tolerated for the sake of appearances and avoided by the other guests. This last thought renders him almost sympathetic.

"Ah! Here's Lyllian!" Lyllian is a Texan flutist with the looks of a young prince of the blood crossed with a cowboy. Under thirty, perfectly distinguished. He immediately impresses Franck as someone superior. They exchange a cordial handshake, warm enough to make both men want to go beyond the ritual pleasantries. Then Evia and Franck greet a few more eminent individuals, lumpish industrialists, senior officials, a famous lawyer, a young Russian harpist, two slick-haired market traders, a B-movie actress, three rather stoned male models, a large man in a burnoose who seems completely out of place, and a with-it novelist who explains to Franck in three minutes why a detective novel must have as its hero a divorced, alcoholic cop always at loggerheads with his superiors. Franck, who inclines more toward the flute player, the Dominican monk, or the man in the burnoose, feels ill at ease among these industrialists, judges, models, and photographers – second-rate thespians trying hard to behave like art lovers. Beauty appeals to them only because of the art market. Without it, the marvels before which they fall into ecstasies would long ago have been abandoned on a public dump. But they have been told how much they are worth. They estimate the value of works instead of looking at them. They show their respect.

"Come, Franck," says Evia, "I'd like to show you our pièce de résistance." She leads him into an adjoining room, in the center of which stands a gigantic marble statue in the classical style, painted a candy pink, its shoulders speckled with bird droppings that make a kind of shawl. "What masterly execution!" crows Mrs. Le Carré.

"And so perfectly in harmony with the rest of the house," adds Franck.

Evia launches into the life and works of the artist – who has one leg and cirrhosis of the liver, and is ranked "somewhere between Michelangelo and Giacometti" – before declaring, almost smugly, that dinner is about to be served. Franck is dreading the moment when he will have to go to the dining table and rub shoulders with this bunch of halfwits, pretend to them that he shares their dilettantish amusements, their seriousness, their enthusiasms, and where there will certainly be a discussion of politics, of reforms, and other idiocies of the same stripe. And he thinks he will have to put up with more insipid diatribes like the one served up by the hotel barman about the so-called barbarous killer of some godforsaken drunk. He knows these people all too well. They come to his office on Madison Avenue, where he hears them expose their petty jealousies and passions. He is familiar with these features, molded into heavy, waxen masks that express nothing but dissipation and death. He knows what they are hiding, what they are trying to flee. He knows the shady dealings they spin, web-like, over the void. He knows all the ways they have of salving their consciences. And the worst is that they believe it! They're sincere!

As they are passing into the dining room, Franck is overcome by nausea. He excuses himself. Bolting the door of the bathroom with its marble-clad floor and walls, he takes out his black mother-of-pearl pocket mirror and sets it down beside the basin. He cuts the cocaine into thin, parallel lines an inch or so apart and snorts them voluptuously through a glass straw. He looks at himself in the mirror, opens his eyes wide, rubs the base of his nose, and then carefully wipes around his nostrils with a tissue.

When he re-emerges, Le Carré's guests are taking their places. Franck sits down opposite Lyllian. Evia and Lance are to his left. Stammering a series of incomprehensible phrases, the red-haired cousin sits down on his right. Franck studies him out of the corner of his eye. He is hanging his head like a dog who fears a beating. Humiliation has probably been part of this man's daily regimen. It most likely began in kindergarten. In school he must have been subjected to all the cruelty and abuse that can be fitted into recess. After school they must have followed him home, calling his name, shouting insults, throwing garbage or stones. If he had been sent away to boarding school, it would have been even worse.

Then Franck's gaze moves to Lyllian, whose good looks disturb him and disrupt his analysis – good looks all the more remarkable when juxtaposed with the ugliness of the physicist and the other guests. Here is a powerful personality, he thinks, brought up in one of those bastions of the delinquent Southern aristocracy. Where did he get his passion for the flute? Was it inherited from his family? The outcome of those evening parties inflicted by the family, when young girls in red dresses coax a wailing cacophony from their poor instruments (leading the men, left to themselves, to speculate that they probably suck better than they blow)? Evia Le Carré would certainly speak of destiny. But Franck doesn't like the word. If chance isn't responsible, you have to admit that fate isn't either.

Further away the models are giggling together, all aquiver. They are discussing an exhibition on Sunbird Avenue that made one of them feel like a dork to be parking a Jaguar when everybody else was driving an Italian sports car or a Bentley. They said they hadn't understood very much, but it was crazy all the same, that Tierce Johns and Peter Paul were there, and the cream of Boston society. (Yes, rich and thick, Franck says to himself.) He then thinks he overhears how they got very high in the washrooms of the hotel where the exhibition was being held, but he can't discover on what – and anyway, why should he care?

On the other side of the table, the novelist is expatiating. Franck hears him say, "But it's not enough to make your detective an alcoholic, ladies and gentlemen, you have to give him a partner; then your cop won't need to talk to himself all the time. Monologues always piss the reader off." The guests roar with laughter while Franck tries to concentrate on Lyllian's words as he tells him about his career – how he came from Texas to the New York Conservatory, and from there to the Boston Philharmonic. He is not pretentious, just conscious of his own worth. What a pleasure to hear him talk, and how he stands out against all these morons around, thinks Franck. He can't help hearing their buzz. The models are relating how they arrived home dead drunk in Cody Roy's limousine, while the celebrated designer smoked a crack pipe and called them "my little elves." The novelist is exposing the secrets of his trade: "It's the urban setting that counts; you've got to have an urban setting! You've got to show them addicts and the working class, underprivileged neighborhoods, dark alleys crawling with rapists and murderers. Believe me, that's what sends them into ecstasies!"

Franck's head is spinning. The background hum of the guests is assailing him more and more acutely. He is in a cold sweat. The novelist goes on: "Above all, you have to be morally irreproachable! When I write I imagine I'm Michael Moore: I ridicule conservatives, the wealthy, I condemn war, racism, and sexism. And don't forget the homophobes! There are more faggots than ever before, so you'd better get them on your side" – he throws a glance at Lyllian – "rather than at your backside." (This sally provokes several belly laughs.)

The models, across the table, are relating the remainder of their evening. "And then, to cap it off, we dragged along

Lili Wagner's daughter, and the little skank was pushing packets of coke out through her pussy."

"You've got to be kidding."

"I swear! It was like a candy dispenser, you know those things that look like plastic guns and you stuff with mints? She shot us out almost half an ounce."

"I don't believe it!"

"Yes, yes, I promise you. I have her number, look!"

"The little slut!"

This conversation risks compromising the Le Carrés. At one end of the table the von Wirts are whispering vehemently. The carrot-top cousin is blushing and wringing his hands. As for Franck, he is torn between his pleasure at seeing the coterie suffer from its own contradictions and his unreserved disgust for the male models with their long thin limbs and airs of devil-may-care druggies.

Looking upset, Evia says, "Thank you, gentlemen, I think we've heard enough." Seizing the initiative, she changes the subject. "Have you read the newspapers? That murder, just a few streets from here… It sends shivers down my spine."

Here we go, thinks Franck. That murder is no worse than the ones your husband pays for.

Mrs. von Wirt speaks up, for the first time since the start of the meal. "Yes, Evia, I saw it in the morning papers… My God, how horrible!"

The models chorus that it's really dreadful the sort of things that go on nowadays, while the novelist acts the expert: he has consulted widely among famous psychiatrists and retired FBI officers in order to draw characters with "a plausible psychological makeup, the key to a successful novel."

"You see," he goes on, "those guys are sick more than anything, very sick. But it's a special kind of sickness, for which the only cure is a lethal injection." He chortles.

"But if they're sick…?" asks Evia, with a hint of reproach in her voice.

"Then you just have to make sure they don't recover – it's that simple!" replies the novelist.

"Do you think he's still around?" asks one of the models.

"Of course he is! Guys like that don't go hunting far from home. You can be sure he's lying low a few blocks away, relishing his deed!"

"My God!" moans Mrs. von Wirt.

The models declare that they are terrified.

"But let me point out," says the man of letters, "that for an artist like myself it does possess a certain interest."

"You're incorrigible!" declares Evia.

For a few moments Franck has been gazing vacantly around the room and at the guests. His conversation with Lyllian has ended. He's wondering if the flutist isn't just as empty as the others after all. Maybe he's just more pleasant to look at.

"The worst of it is," Mr. von Wirt goes on, "that the killer didn't take anything! Not a thing! He left a wallet with more than a hundred dollars in it. What about that? It makes no sense! What do you make of it?"

Abruptly, Franck turns toward him and looks him in the eye. "Well, I make of it that he's an honest man."

Evia throws him an astounded glance, while her husband lowers his head, and the guests' chatter stops. Only the novelist sneers, "You'll have to explain your thinking!"

"What I mean is that his act was as spontaneous as it was disinterested. Just think, a man who's not calculating – I find that refreshing."

"Franck, are you serious?"

"All the same," Le Carré puts in, "the guy will be entitled to a good long vacation when they get their hands on him!"

And what about you? thinks Franck.

"Oh, but it's not at all sure they'll ever get their hands on him!" declares the novelist. "Do you know the percentage of murders that remain unsolved?"

"Do you think he'll do it again?" asks Evia.

"No doubt about it! But where? And when? No one can say. Sometimes brutes like that can lie low for years! But they always end by killing again—"

"It's dreadful!"

"Dreadful!" echo the models.

"It's life," summarizes the novelist.

Franck is not unhappy to have distressed the company. The models gaze at him timidly, half in admiration, half in disgust. The novelist seems to consider him a kindred spirit. Only Lyllian keeps his eyes lowered.

"You don't agree?" Franck asks him.

"The thing is… The way I see things…"

"It's wrong to kill your neighbor?"

"Do you find that ridiculous?"

"No, I find it charming. It's just that I think there are certain people you *can* kill."

"You mean criminals, for instance?"

"I mean people who get in your way. You have to remove obstacles from your path, precisely because they are obstacles. It's only later that justice and human rights come into play."

"But what about the old guy… The old guy, apparently, had never done anything."

"Maybe he just became an obstacle to someone… And anyway, between you and me, that old guy wasn't necessarily an angel… We're much too quick to make saints of the dead. What's to say that he'd never killed anyone? Committed rape? Spied on his granddaughter in the shower? Who's to know? Videoed her? Then sold the files? I—"

"So you dream of the gallows while smoking your hookah," says Lyllian with a smile.

"Do people really read Baudelaire in Dallas?"

"No, either you're poor, in which case you drink and murder someone, or rich, in which case you drink and kill yourself."

Franck laughs. "But not you!"

"But not me."

"I like you. I like unusual people."

"Like the killer?"

"No. He does break the monotony, there's no denying it. But maybe he's very ordinary. An ordinary man is above all someone predictable, decipherable, tragic. Someone as pitiful as he's repugnant."

"And I'm neither pitiful nor repugnant?"

"No. You should have died of an overdose halfway between a sugar refinery and a cotton field. I think you haven't come out of it too badly" – he lowers his voice and leans toward Lyllian – "as long as you don't compromise yourself too often at dos like this one."

Just then the novelist leans toward Evia. "I think our two lovebirds are going to end up in the same nest." The models whisper together about inviting them to a "Special K party" on Hammer Street that evening.

"You're right, but I find a kind of warmth here—"

"Compared to your family in Texas?"

"Yes… And I find people who can understand me, that I can talk to—"

"Think again! You can't talk to these people."

"I don't deny that sometimes that's true…"

"If they offer you money, take it. But don't look up to them."

"You're being hard, Franck."

"Worse! All things considered, I prefer truckers, or longshoremen. They let you know right away that they don't give a damn about you. They don't waste any time spouting or spinning yarns."

"So basically, where ordinariness is concerned, or idiocy, you'd rather be left in peace?"

The novelist is whispering in Evia's ear: "I hope they'll be able to restrain themselves till they leave… What passion!"

The models are tittering more than ever, nudging one another, and declaring that those two would most definitely fit in at their party.

"Yes, you could say that my peace and quiet are important to me."

"Enough to kill for?" asks Lyllian.

"Enough to kill for."

"At least *you*'re not ordinary."

A veil of melancholy comes over Franck's eyes. "I'd like to be sure of it, Lyllian."

Professor Caron seems to be listening to the conversation with considerable interest. But he says nothing, and no one speaks to him.

"Why do you doubt it?"

Several seconds of silence.

"I'd rather talk about it some other time," answers Franck, excusing himself, rising, and making for the bathroom.

"Ah! There you are! You can be sure the other one will follow him," exults the novelist. The models look at one another knowingly.

But the other one doesn't follow him. In the suffocating marble bathroom Franck takes out his mirror and recommences the same ritual as before, slightly increasing the dose. He snorts the powder slowly, almost grain by grain. Then he puts his straw away and stares at himself in the mirror. He examines his reflection for a few minutes, absorbed in his own gaze, then makes a face at himself, unlocks the door, and returns to his place.

When Franck leaves the mansion, it is past four o'clock. Darkness is beginning to fall. Lyllian had left a few minutes earlier, after accepting the models' invitation. Franck feels weary and depressed. Lance Le Carré shakes his hand almost warmly, and Evia is all over him. The with-it novelist and the models extort an embrace from him and loudly express their regret that they won't see him later. As for Professor Caron, he seems to hesitate. He approaches Franck and timidly informs him that he hopes to see him soon again, that he would like to know him better. He only had to talk to me during lunch, thinks Franck. Why did he say nothing? Why do I have the impression that he was following me yesterday? And that shifty, downcast expression of his... What a strange character! Who would have thought it? Two unusual people in a backwater like this!

He says goodbye to the company at large, crosses the avenue flanked with cypress trees, gets into the 300C, and drives away.

11

Sinatra is making the speakers in the Ford squad car vibrate: "My Kind of Town."

"Know what drives me crazy?" asks the sheriff. "It's feeling that what we do is useless ..."

"That we're just a drop in the ocean, you mean?"

McCarthy nods. "Yes, that we get out of bed every morning remembering a few scraps of youthful idealism, the oath we've taken, serving the citizens, the country, and then seeing that for every guy we arrest three others come out of the woodwork. I sometimes feel I'm swimming against the current, and I'm not strong enough."

"And yet you keep going. Otherwise, Sheriff, you and me wouldn't be digging up dirt, getting stuck with interrogations that lead nowhere, and picking up the mutilated bodies of old guys on street corners."

Below Interstate 93, the ocean reflects the pale afternoon sun. Gomez is lost in it for a few moments, and then adds, "We're the ones who do the dirty work, you and me; we often wish we were in a different place, but we get out of bed every morning all the same."

McCarthy nods and sighs, "Yes, but we do have something else..." The sheriff is shaking. He brings his hand to his heart and then back to the steering wheel. He completes the sentence: "Family."

"Sure, that's something…"

"That's what gives meaning."

He thinks of the inhabitants of the Bellams, the drunks, the lost souls, the utterly empty ones. For them, waking up in the morning, getting out of bed, and dressing doesn't have much more meaning than dying, or killing someone. These are the people Gomez and McCarthy have to deal with every day in the Bellams, wherever in Watertown, down dark alleys. He knows them. He has heard them say under questioning that they don't care about anything and describe how apathetic, how indifferent they feel. Beating up an old woman or lighting a joint, killing themselves or opening a can of Coke, it's all the same to them. The sheriff and his deputy have set themselves an objective they call Justice. That is the path they follow, that guides and inspires them; what they do has a reason. The ones that sit in the back of the Ford squad car only act by instinct. They have no principles, no ideals. They have only themselves, and the dark – which are sometimes one and the same.

Yet not everything seemed foreordained. They had prospects. They were meant (their parents used to say) for a brilliant career, to attend the best schools, to have a position in life. Life would smile on them. The angels, heaven itself, would welcome them. They were promised a happy life! A varied one! They had a winning streak that lasted fifteen, twenty, sometimes thirty years. And then they lost. When, exactly? It's not easy to say.

Barney Henderson, "Cousin Bart," was among those who seemed to show great promise. He had a quick intelligence, and his parents were predicting the moon for him even before he could read or count. The family bled itself almost white to allow him to attend a decent college. Barney lived up to expectations. He was serious, determined – not especially brilliant, but he made up for his lack of genius by hard work. He went on to art school, and then achieved a measure of success, first in New York and later in Europe. He never became an important painter, yet he was able to earn some recognition and enough money to buy a studio beside the sea south of Boston, not far from Duxbury. At first he was content there. He would go painting in the evening, along the seashore. The neighborhood kids called him "The Old Man and the Sea." Then regrets began to accumulate, a swarm of tiny wounds to his pride. His body grew tired. He was losing his grip on life, on hope. As the years went by he became the old man and the six-pack, the old man and the stupid program on MTV, and finally the old man and the weekly visits to a state clinic to pee in a beaker. Nowadays he hardly ever paints. He pays his rent, and his bills. Then, at night, he sheds a few tears.

"You think Barney knows something?" asks Gomez.

"I've no idea, but young Julia says her grandfather grew close to him over the past few months and used to visit him often."

"And Laura Henderson?"

"Maybe she's in Philly… Apparently she has a girlfriend living there. Hendrix is looking into it."

"And Barney, what are we hoping to get from him?"

"Maybe a crack in the apparently blank wall of Jimmy's existence."

Gomez sighs. "It was me drew up the inventory of his truck and his apartment. Frankly, if there is any crack... What I mean is, the guy had to have some faults, some secrets, a few small skeletons in his closet, but at first sight there was nothing that would point to anything criminal, or suggest that—"

"Yes, but the thing is, there was a crime."

Barney Henderson's house, from outside, gives the impression of a certain elegance – despite the grass growing up to the windowsills and the paint mostly flaked off the façade. Standing less than a hundred yards from the ocean, in a neighborhood where opulent houses flourish, it does confer a certain standing on its occupant: the mail carrier calls him respectfully "Mr. Henderson" and the home-care nurse (a psychotic African-American woman) has already made him three offers of marriage, two for herself and one on behalf of her daughter.

But once you go inside, the illusion crumbles. The main room, a kind of sitting/dining room, seems to have been laid waste by one of those storms that develop over the sea: it's a real catastrophe, a local apocalypse sponsored by Budweiser. The furniture is decaying and collapsing onto the floor, the curtains are filthy and sagging, as are the lampshades; bottles and scraps of food litter the ground. In the middle of it all, under an incredible farrago of blankets, moth-eaten shawls, and greasy knee blankets, sits Barney Henderson, tiny, puny, and bent, who expels three loud belches before the two officers can extract a word from him.

"Enemies? Why would my cousin have had enemies?"

"That's for you to tell us, Mr. Henderson," Gomez interjects.

"What kind of enemy do you think he could have had, apart from his daughter's screw? They're a fine pair of good-for-nothings."

"So, apart from Alexander Marshall, you can't think of anyone that might have done this thing?"

Barney shakes his head.

"Did your cousin ever talk to you about any problems or concerns he might have had?"

"Yeah, he hadn't been peeing too good of late, but mind you it was a lot better than me. Do you know, the doctor told me—"

Gomez interrupts. "And apart from his health?"

Henderson reflects. His little red-rimmed eyes scrutinize the curtains, hoping to find an answer. "Maybe dough."

"Your cousin had money problems?"

"Oh, who doesn't! Tell me, how great do you feel toward the end of the month yourself?" He is shaking. He flies into a rage. "For God's sake, for a few years now it's really been going down the tubes for everyone. Don't you see the crap that's going on? And the assholes that line their pockets a thousand times over? Huh? And my cousin must have felt it too!"

The sheriff intervenes, with a smile. "You're quite right, Mr. Henderson, it's not easy for anyone. But what we'd like to know is if your cousin had contracted any debts, developed a taste for gambling, or anything like that..."

Barney rubs his chin, gives a long belch, and then answers, "There was the girl..."

"You mean Julia?" asks Gomez.

"Right! Jim's head has been full of all kinds of fancy notions about her this last while. He said he wanted to take her into his place, send her to a good school, pay for piano lessons for her, and bullshit like that..." With a circular wave of his hand, he shows his living room. "You see what that leads to?"

"And he found a solution?"

"No! What do you think? His damfool daughter cleaned him out long ago! He hardly had enough to put gas in his truck."

Gomez pauses for a moment. He knows about those kinds of situations, desires, "fancies." He too would like his daughter to be able to attend a decent school where they still teach math and the history of the United States, where you can eat the cafeteria food without needing to see the doctor afterward. He knows what it is to lack means. To slave away the whole week to earn a pension and a few minor pleasures, with the permanent sharp, stinging feeling that you're missing out on something. He glances at the sheriff, who nods to him to continue.

"Okay, Barney. Now tell me, did Jimmy Henderson come to see you often before he died?"

Barney is startled. He spits on the floor and looks at them as if he is out of his mind. "Huh? Hold on now, guys, you don't think it was me sliced him up?"

"No, Mr. Henderson." The sheriff takes over. "It's just

that we have to have a more precise impression of the life your cousin was leading at the time of his death."

Barney nods. "Yeah, well, Jim did come quite often… Maybe once a month."

"And why exactly did he come to see you?"

"Why exactly? Well… to drink a beer, to chat, a second beer, things like that, see?"

"And he came all the way from Boston just to see you?"

"So I'm not worth the trip, is that what you're saying?"

Since they got there the deputy has indeed been telling himself that Barney Henderson wasn't worth the trip. He wonders what can make a man seek such company, take any pleasure in seeing someone wasting away like that, dying a slow death – the worst kind – from thwarted pride and accumulated regrets. Even long enough to drink a beer is too much already, he thinks.

"Please understand my colleague, Mr. Henderson, he's asking a legitimate question. After all, your cousin was elderly, older than you, so naturally we have to wonder what was the purpose of his trips…"

"It seems that when you get older you like a good chat."

The sheriff nods. "And besides," continues Barney, "old buddies are dying all around us, so you start drawing little crosses on your old school yearbooks, and it's only natural to want to get closer to your distant cousins, to patch things up between you and bring them a beer now and again… Is there any harm in that?"

Gomez smiles, "None at all, Mr. Henderson."

Old Barney smiles too, a wan, weary smile.

"Mr. Henderson, are you quite sure your cousin used to come to Duxbury just to see you?"

"Well, no!" exclaims Barney.

"So what did he come to do around here, then?" asks Gomez.

"Shopping, I think, yeah, stuff for hunting, or fishing."

"Fishing?"

"That was his latest craze. He would go off fishing in Canada, to a buddy's cottage, or else in Vermont."

"So then he came to buy fishing tackle?"

"That's what I said."

"Do you have an address?"

"Are you a fisherman too?" Then, noticing the renewed interest in the policemen's faces, Barney quickly adds, "No, not me. I'm not interested in fish. Time was I painted the sea, and I did a hell of a job. But I never took the trouble to pull its denizens out from the waves in order to cut out their guts."

"Thank you, Mr. Henderson."

"You're welcome! Turn out the light as you go."

The sheriff and his deputy stand up. They can still hear him belching in the dark as they go out, closing the door behind them.

12

The Foxtraps neighborhood has a peaceful reputation. Modest townhouses separated by immaculate lawns extend along Peacock Street and Mount Auburn. The gardens are embellished with stainless steel barbecues, plastic tables and chairs, varnished wooden kennels, and so-called "child-safe" swings. Paul McCarthy's house is at 52 Peacock Street. His immediate neighbor is a door-to-door dishwasher salesman, while the neighbor opposite, a recent retiree, devotes his time to carving pumpkins – an art practiced by his mother before him. Of all the inhabitants of the Foxtraps, McCarthy is the one whose job is considered the most exciting and different. Sometimes the neighbors chat from their doorsteps or at the celebrated neighborhood barbecues. In the simplicity of tradition, church, and family, the sheriff reflects, these solid citizens spend their days often peacefully, occasionally disturbed, but always honorably. Here, people do what they need to stay alive, he thinks. The stability of the neighborhood strikes him all the more in that he spends his days immersed in its exact opposite: the perpetual, potential slide into the atmosphere of a muffled, interminable bomb-blast. It is an endless succession of drunken brawls, abusive husbands, surly traffickers, and corpses to step over. When he takes off his uniform, says goodbye to Gomez and Jaspers, and exchanges the Ford squad car for his gray Grand Marquis, he is glad to extract himself from the chaos and filth and hug his wife and children – and also embrace the sweetness of an ordered existence. He knows that in the Bellams or Dorchester people think he lives on easy street, that he is privileged; he knows he is a laughingstock for the with-it, bohemian circles who take pleasure in mocking family values, barbecues, slippers, and dog kennels. But the former ones have never had any choice, and experience has taught the sheriff that very few among the needy working-class people who live in the Bellams would, if they had the option, refuse the luxury of a tranquil existence and a perfect lawn. McCarthy is sure that even among the most depraved, the utterly vicious, those ravaged to the marrow, many long for the quiet life of the Foxtraps. As for the artists and dilettantes, the sheriff thinks it would do them good to be confronted, just once, with a drug-hungry amphetamine addict threatening them with a gun; it would sharpen their senses and knock a few ideas into their skulls.

When he comes home from work in the evening, his wife, two daughters and a polished hardwood floor are there to welcome him. The walls are hung with watercolors that he paints in his spare time, "with no pretensions." The furniture is sober, light in color, and constitutes a functional, harmonious ensemble which leads guests to comment that the McCarthys "have taste." The kitchen, living room, and a small dining room occupy the ground floor. The bedrooms are upstairs, along with a den where the sheriff mulls over his current cases or deals with the tasks related to his activities with the Church of the Redemption. That is where he is when Jaspers calls.

"McCarthy."

"Good evening, Sheriff. Sorry to disturb you."

"You're not disturbing me."

"I've checked on Jimmy Henderson's address book like you asked."

"Did you find anything?"

"Among the phone numbers listed, just two are connected to an address south of Roxbury."

"Go on."

"One belongs to a certain Karen Haye, a retired social worker living in South Roxbury."

McCarthy takes a note of it.

"The other one was under the initials 'B. H.,' but it's the number of a fitness club, The Muscles of Love, in Fort Owl."

"Thanks for that."

Without hanging up the phone, McCarthy is ruminating.

"Will that be all, Sheriff?"

"Just one thing…"

"Yes?"

"Tell me, do you know a lot of retirees in their seventies with a prostate problem who are willing to drive for an hour just to work out in a fitness club?"

Jaspers laughs. "Very few, come to think of it."

"Then ask his telephone company to send us a list of his calls during, let's say, the past three months. Tell them it's urgent. And see what you can find out about that fitness club."

*

At the dinner table, the sheriff, with eyes closed, is just finishing saying grace, holding his wife and one of his daughters by the hand. Then he opens his eyes, raises his head, and smiles. He says "Amen!" in a loud voice. The rest of the family choruses "Amen!" in response, and then "Enjoy!" Carefully, he begins to carve the meat. "Order is meaning," he sometimes says. And he is terribly afraid of losing that meaning, of letting things slide. Grounded in habit and ritual, and certain he is acting each day for the good of others – even if it is sometimes difficult and seems useless – he fends off despair and insanity, the monsters that overwhelmed both his father and mother.

Doubtless their meals aren't elaborate – just like the room they are in, its cream-painted walls graced only by two small watercolors and a plain wooden crucifix, just like the rest of the house, just like the rest of the neighborhood, but which creates an environment spacious enough to allow one to breathe easily yet small enough not to get lost in. "Knowing where things are, knowing where you are; that's what happiness is," he sometimes says to his wife when they are in bed.

Charlene McCarthy clears her throat before asking her husband, "What kind of a day did you have? We read about that awful business in the newspapers—"

The sheriff signals to her to go no further, and winks.

"They know very well what's going on, Paul. In town it's the only thing folks are talking about!"

"You know, you and the children are like the press – I can't tell you anything!"

Everyone laughs wholeheartedly.

"Can the killer really be this drug-starved addict the papers talk about?"

"Frankly, I've no idea... Gomez has his doubts."

"And you?"

"I don't know what to think anymore. We may have another line of inquiry... But I've seen the unexpected so often – no, in fact *not* the unexpected, but the entirely expected – that I can't say anything."

He'd like to say more. He'd like to confide his doubts about Alexander Marshall's guilt to his wife, and tell her too how often they've said of someone, "It can't be him; that would be too obvious," when it did turn out in the end that the individual was indeed responsible. If Alexander Marshall is a scumbag, he may be enough of one to kill someone and then come back to mutilate the corpse, and even forget to take the money. Appearances are not always deceptive. Sometimes they are even all that's left of reality.

"Dad, what will you do with the bad man when you find him?"

"I'll arrest him, honey, the way I always do."

"And if he doesn't want to go along?"

"He won't have any choice! When you do bad things to people, you've got to go to prison."

"And what's it like in prison?"

The sheriff hesitates before answering. He thinks of his last visit to Norfolk County Jail, looking at that frail adolescent in the infirmary, his entire face a bloody mess.

"It's not nice."

In the meantime, he eats. Charlene eats. The children too. They utter a few words, they smile. They don't laugh out loud; they are accustomed instead to a warm, mellow, precious joy – the joy of being together under the same roof. So let the world with its pageant of the sick, the failures, and the ravaged remain on the doorstep. They are together, they are happy, and they show it with restrained gestures that are imperceptible from the outside.

13

Parked on Peacock Street with the detachable butt of his Steyr TMP pressed to his shoulder, Franck lines up McCarthy in his sights, then his wife, then each of his daughters. For him, this pastoral scene, with its sterile setting, is a scandal. Of course, it is what he expected. He had met the sheriff at the Church of the Redemption. But at the time the music, indifferent though it was, lent a kind of grandeur, a beauty, to people and things. Here, in the silence, in the night, the neat rows of little white houses fill his heart with a combination of gloom and disgust. It would be doing them a favor to shoot them, he thinks. He'd be sparing them the degradation of growing old in this cesspit full of angels and incense fumes; he'd be destroying this genre painting by a minor master, gashed with forced smiles. He strokes the barrel of his machine pistol. Not a single movement of the family escapes him. Right now the sheriff is scolding his daughter. Probably for botching some school work, unless it's for peeing in a stoup or sticking a twig up a frog's anus, thinks Franck. There follows an animated discussion on the transcendence of morality, or some garbage like that. A skinny, gnarled man, preceded by his three dogs, crosses his field of vision. Franck watches him fade into the night and then reemerge at intervals under the streetlights which facilitate the Neighborhood Watch program that is such a valued aspect of American residential neighborhoods, those great, morbid (but anesthetized) growths dotted with townhomes, tiny yards, and white mailboxes that exist all across North America, even as far as Alaska and Canada's Northwest Territories.

When Paul McCarthy rises to answer the phone, Franck lays his gun on the seat and puts on his earphones. He hears the sheriff answer, then a man's voice saying, "It's Jaspers, Sheriff. I've found out more about our fitness club."

"I'm listening."

"It's owned by Lance Le Carré, but it's managed by a guy called Tom Lord, who was jailed for rape at the end of the 1980s. His latest conviction goes back to 2010, when he was busted with his pockets full of crystal meth. He was also very much involved in the porn movie business."

"Involved how?"

"As an actor. His specialty was violent fellatio – you get that? But he also dabbled in comedy... For example, a trilogy where he had himself sodomized with the prosthesis of a guy who—"

"Skip it—"

"His stage name is Wild Bill Hiscock."

"B. H.!" exclaimed McCarthy, "like in old Jim's daybook."

"Exactly, chief."

"We'll call on him tomorrow morning. Anything else?"

"Yes, indeed. The narcs are on his case too."

"What do you mean?"

"Apparently there's an investigation underway... Drug dealing. They think the fitness club is a kind of transfer

86

depot, where the goods are shifted from the suppliers to the dealers. Le Carré is a suspect."

The sheriff groans. "And what about the dealers?"

"Oh, a whole lot of guys…"

McCarthy reflects for a few moments. "Poor guys beaten down by life, in need of a little dough, for example?"

"Yeah, something like that."

"So they're afraid that with our big boots we're going to mess up their operation?"

The sheriff reflects. He feels a strong desire to hold off, to give the narcs enough time, and to bring down Le Carré, who up to now no one has been able to touch. But murder is murder, and given the media buzz about this one, it wouldn't look good to delay… What's more, he thinks, Le Carré works with so many sub-dealers that they'll never be able to lay a finger on him.

"Tell the narcs they've got the whole night if they want to score an arrest. We won't do anything till tomorrow morning."

"Understood, chief. Anything else?"

"Meeting at ten with everybody. Good night."

Franck removes his earphones. He is still observing the McCarthy home. The sheriff seems to have gone upstairs (there's a light in his office). His wife goes across the living room. The kids have vanished. Their little world has dispersed, he thinks, each gone off to bed to struggle with their little anxieties. Unless they no longer even have enough strength, enough spirit to feel any anxiety? An impulse? Vertigo? Not to be anything more than little tenderly wrapped mummies, busy petrifying under their bandages, slowly going stiff in their open tomb – until some blow of fate intervenes, sealing down the lid and blocking the opening. Miserable robots, with souls as impoverished as their actions, condemned to the monotony of a sterile existence composed of indifference and repetition.

He stows the Steyr TMP and the earphones in the glove compartment. Peacock Street is now deserted. As he drives off he connects his hands-free phone. It rings three times before she answers.

"Good evening, Franck! It's nice to hear from you."

"Good evening, Mariella! I didn't wake you?"

"I was just dozing, don't worry. Can I do something for you?"

"Well, you see, I'm on a new case."

"One that will earn us a pretty sum, I hope…"

"Not a single dollar! It's just a curious business, if I can call it that."

"And I suppose that's an excellent reason to give it priority, even if everything else has to suffer…"

Franck laughs. "Bull's-eye as usual!"

"So what do you want?"

"Two things… First, I need you to send me the file on a low-level dealer called Bill Hiscock. You'll find him under Le Carré. Hiscock works for him."

"Perfect. I'll send you the file within the half-hour. But you said you needed a second bit of information?"

Stopping at a red light on Lindman Street, Franck notices three guys busily beating up another between two garbage bins, kicking him as he lies on the ground.

"Yes. I need information about a Professor Ernest Caron, a physicist. He's Lance Le Carré's cousin. He doesn't teach anymore. I'd like to know why."

The guy on the ground has stopped moving. One of the three attackers opens his fly and starts to urinate on him. "I see. I'll take a look in the database."

"Thanks!"

He drives on.

14

Fretfully, Franck is turning the pages of the Péladan book. The room is thick with cigarette smoke, gloom, and ammonia vapor. The tiny grains of coke are burning along the white Davidoff. "*The study of passion in periods of decadence almost always discovers an illogical, irrational, and absurd determinism underlying psychic phenomena. In those historical moments when a civilization is nearing its end, the principal reality is a nauseous condition of the soul and, especially among the upper classes, a weariness of existence. Then, consciously, deliberately, lives are ruined, intelligence is frittered away, and evil becomes loved for its own sake.*" Franck closes his eyes. He pulls on his cigarette. The hint of a smile appears at the corners of his mouth. The practice of evil for its own sake, he reflects, is always better than those animated corpses called sheriffs and parish secretaries, who fancy they do good for its own sake! These fools dripping with piety mistake stumbling for kneeling.

Someone knocks on the door. Franck sets down the book and stubs out his cigarette. He leaps to his feet.

"Just a moment, please," he says loudly, trying to sound cheerful and amiable. Quickly he dons his jacket and collects his machine pistol from the nightstand. He tiptoes over to the door and, with the gun at his side, ready to fire, looks through the peephole. Then he walks back and stows the Steyr TMP in his bag. When he opens the door, the bestselling author of crime novels is standing there, wearing a broad smile.

"Hi!" he exclaims.

Franck doesn't react. He stares at him.

"Surprised to see me?"

"Not really. I just wonder how you were able to find my room."

"Ha ha! Mystery!" (He winks.) "You didn't know we were staying in the same hotel?"

"No, I thought you lived in Boston."

"I'm from Long Island."

Another silence from Franck.

"I thought you wouldn't be going to that party on Hammer Street. That sort of thing is okay for the young – they're having new experiences, they're getting stoned, right? That's just natural. But it's not for us! So I thought, since we're both literary guys and obviously have the same sense of humor, the two of us could share a few drinks in the bar, if you've nothing else planned…"

"I'm not a literary guy, and I don't have the same sense of humor as you at all… But I accept your invitation. Give me ten minutes and I'll join you."

"That's great, Franck! Great!" (He gives him another wink.) "I'll wait for you in the bar."

Franck locks the door. Then he stows the Péladan in the nightstand, changes his shirt, fills his cigarette case, and pockets the butterfly knife. What does that moron want with me? he thinks. Is he really counting on spending the evening with me? Or is it a trap set by Le Carré? Franck didn't get the impression that the novelist was carrying a weapon, nor even that he would be capable of using a gun. But it's wiser to take precautions.

The bar is as cold and impersonal as the day before. The people sitting in it have a different veneer, but the wood is the same. Wholesalers, traders, portfolio managers, former celebrities, and the very wealthy – with, as if to confound expectations, a stunning young woman and a seductive young man every so often. The bestselling novelist is at a table off on its own, holding his head down, in the attitude of someone afraid of being recognized. One thing's sure, thinks Franck. If this guy is supposed to kill me, I've nothing to worry about. He goes over to him, smiling. "I hope I didn't keep you waiting too long!"

"Franck!" (The novelist roars with laughter, for no apparent reason.) "Not at all! That was fast! Thanks for coming. Life in Boston can be pretty grim if you're in poor company."

You're telling me! thinks Franck.

The other man continues, "So, what will we have? I've good memories of the burgundy."

"Okay, let's have some red!"

He signals to the waiter. "Some burgundy, my friend." Then, to Franck, "Just imagine, I only drink wine occasionally. Well, what can you do? I grew up the hard way: Budweiser and Molson were our household gods."

Franck smiles, and then murmurs, "May I ask you an embarrassing question…?"

The novelist leans forward, with a complicit air. "Anything you like!"

"Well," says Franck, "I've forgotten your name."

The stout novelist is disconcerted. For a celebrity accustomed to people whispering as he goes by, this supposedly cultured guy's question is disconcerting. Yet he forces a smile, to put on a good face for this schnook.

"I'm James Ellsor."

Yes, Franck recalls. James Ellsor, displayed prominently in every bookstore, whose every book is an event, whose books sell in the hundred thousands, and who had recently been caught out in a hilarious transgression when a journalist noticed that he would regularly log on to Amazon to write positive reviews of his own books while brutally denigrating those of his fellow writers.

Franck nods. "Yes, I recognize the name."

Amazing! thinks the novelist. "You've never read me?"

"Not yet."

"Maybe you're not a big reader…"

"Not at all, I confess. But I'm delighted to discuss literature whenever the opportunity arises, especially with a man of taste."

Ellsor guffaws. "You see! I was sure we'd get on like a house on fire!"

The waiter pours two glasses of wine.

"To our meeting!"

"To our meeting!" echoes Franck.

Ellsor knocks back half his glass in a single gulp, before his little bloodshot eyes return to Franck. "And what do you read, if it's not indiscreet to ask?"

"At the moment I'm reading Péladan."

"Péla-who?"

"Péladan."

"A big seller?"

"Anything but, very probably."

"Ah, I see, he's one of those obscure French writers who split every hair and spend their time chasing their tails for the benefit of the hundred or so nutcases brave enough to read them. Pardon my candor!"

"You're very astute."

"At the same time, the French prefer to read us because we know what a real novel is: something with a spark, action-packed, that makes you sweat a bit. Powerful writing! Something that makes you drop your work, sacrifice your spare time and coffee breaks to get back to reading us. We Americans have a talent for addiction!"

Seeing the novelist's small, reddish eyes and the slightly yellow circles beneath them, Franck tells himself that as far as that goes he must know what he's talking about.

Ellsor goes on: "A book has to be red-hot! Otherwise, what do you have? It drops from people's hands, they put it away and never come back to it. Have you ever read a French author who really transports you?"

"I can assure you I have—"

"Allow me to doubt it!"

Franck realizes that his fears were unfounded. This guy is just a crackpot who wants to yammer on interminably. He'll soliloquize like that for a few hours, oblivious to the fact that there is someone sitting opposite, and find himself alone at closing time with no clue about what has happened.

"Do you know the trick for making readers believe in your novel?"

Franck doesn't bother to reply.

"All you have to do is write every twenty pages or so 'This isn't a movie,' or 'This is no soap opera, this is real life,' that kind of thing. Then the reader tells himself that this guy has *cojones*, he's not just a scribbler; he believes in your characters, in the world of your novel, whatever! Just remember, 'It's not like in books'; that's all you need!" Ellsor takes another sip of red wine. He looks at the ceiling, apparently absorbed, almost melancholy. "There are two tyrannical bitches for a writer—"

"Publishers?" suggests the detective, not thinking much about it, and looking elsewhere.

"No, my friend, those guys make a pile of money; it's clear, it's clean, and that's it. I'm talking about worse, real tyranny, actual fascism: it's readers! Yes, siree! Surprised?"

"Not really—"

"You can't imagine how many dickheads turn up at my book signings to tell me how I should have written my book, how I should write the next one, and what I'm supposed to be like as a person. Then they give me their blessing! They congratulate me on remaining modest, on preserving my humility, they say. Humility, that's what really tickles them. They can't get over it that I don't attack them, that I say 'hi' to them, that I call them Mr. this or that. But sometimes they give me a hard time. Why? I haven't a clue! They tell me I'm too this, too that, whatever! Assholes that have never written a book, never achieved anything in their whole lives, come and give me a hard time – me, that sells four hundred thousand copies a clip! Can they be serious?" He takes a deep breath, and goes on. "The second bitch is the critics."

Franck nods.

"They're a pack of rabid dogs; you're never good enough for them; you've never proved yourself enough. That's their great obsession: that you prove yourself! They expect something of you, you see? So you've got to show them you can live up to their expectations. And then they've the arrogance of guys that have read everything, heard everything, for whom there's nothing new under the sun."

"It's tough," admits Franck, remembering a pamphlet by Théophile Gautier attacking journalists.

"But you don't know the worst! On top of it all, those pit bulls are proud as peacocks!"

"You're describing a zoo!"

Ellsor roars with laughter. "Look, if you're hoping to please the Boston critics, for instance, you should never set a book in Boston. What jingoists! What chauvinists! They'll attribute the lowest of motives to you, catch you out on insignificant details, accuse you of drawing a caricature. On the other hand, in LA, in San Francisco, in Vancouver, they'll praise you to the skies! Crown you with laurels! They'll find you've 'hit just the right note,' that it's 'striking panic realism,' that you've 'given a real sense of the Eastern Seaboard,' that you've 'shown it in all its complexity,' and a bucketful of praise you won't even know what to make of."

Franck, finding this diatribe quite sensible, risks joining the conversation. "So you're saying that unless you're going to be full of praise, you should only write about far-off places?"

"Ah! You're a treat, Franck! That's exactly it! Set the thing in Kingman, Arizona. Paint a really nasty scene, with addicts in every house, violence, fanaticism, a touch of incest. Who's going to hold it against you? Honestly, do you know a lot of critics living in Kingman, Arizona? Waiter, another bottle for my friend and myself!"

Ellsor leans toward Franck, and says, in a confidential tone, "Do you know what really sells these days? The dismembered bodies of young girls."

"The dismembered bodies of young girls?" repeats Franck.

"Yessiree! Stolen childhood and all that crap. You've no idea how well that sells! All the bestsellers of these past few years are about young girls chopped to bits. Now explain that to me! Are the authors perverts? The readers? Maybe a publishers' niche? I haven't a clue."

Franck nods, then yawns and says, "Forgive me if I leave you for a few moments."

Ellsor titters and winks. "Go easy now, Franck! Don't overdo it!"

Franck smiles as he heads for the washroom.

James Ellsor finishes his own glass of burgundy and also Franck's (since that druggie's never coming back from the john, he thinks). Then he heads for the elevators. A young, immaculately uniformed flunky is acting as elevator attendant – though guests only have to press the "up" button.

"Will this damfool machine of yours not go any faster?" Ellsor finally yells at the attendant, as they reach the fourteenth floor.

Unflustered, he merely answers, "Just a few moments more, sir."

Ellsor lets out a heavy sigh. He's angry that Franck has abandoned him. How can the guy have the gall to take French leave like that while he, James Ellsor, whose books sell four hundred thousand copies, who has entire pages devoted to him in the *Times*, and a fan club numbering over twelve thousand active members, does him the honor of inviting him to his table? This upstart, whom he has secretly baptized The Vaselined Faggot from the Café de Paris, has left him in a fury.

He doesn't tip the lift attendant, and when he finally reaches his room, curses on realizing he forgot to lock the door. He switches on the light, takes a laptop from his suitcase, opens it, lowers the blinds, and unbuttons his shirt. As soon as Windows has finished loading, he opens an MP4 file entitled "Underage Runaway Hotties," grabs a bottle of champagne from the fridge, pours himself a glass, and sheds his trousers. Just as he is ready to stretch out on the bed, he hears a creak. Before he has time to turn around, an arm passes under his chin, jerking his head back, and he feels a blade against his throat.

"I'm sorry," whispers a voice. "It took me a bit longer—"

"Franck! What—"

"Don't call out, or you're a dead man."

The novelist keeps quiet, barely uttering a squeak; he is sweating profusely.

"Shush, James, shush—"

"Stop this, Franck, you're nuts!"

"Worse than that!"

"For God's sake, what do you want? Tell me what you want!"

"What do I want? Come on now, surely you can guess!"

"I've got money, there, in my suitcase. Take it, my computer, my dope, everything. I won't breathe a word! I swear! I won't breathe a word!"

"I just want to read to you, my friend. It means a lot to me."

Ellsor is literally peeing his pants. Franck's nostrils are full of the stench of urine. In the mirror, he watches the novelist's ashen, sweating head. He can feel him trembling in his embrace, with the blade of the butterfly knife resting on the carotid artery.

"Have you got one of your books here?"

"In my bag! In my bag!" yelps Ellsor, terrorized.

"Thanks." Yet Franck doesn't relax his hold.

"Let me go! Please—"

"No, James, I'm afraid that's not possible..."

Ellsor is choking on his own spittle.

Franck leans close to his ear, and murmurs, "I only read dead authors."

The novelist has finished urinating. He no longer tries to resist. He merely utters a gentle moan. They remain like that for about fifteen seconds. The point of the knife moves over the writer's throat, exerting no pressure, leaving no trace. The moans continue. The smell of urine. Then, suddenly, Franck relaxes his grasp and pushes Ellsor onto the bed. He pockets the knife.

Standing in the middle of the room, the detective is perfectly calm and smiling. "Mr. Ellsor, I'm really sorry if my manners weren't to your liking. I just wanted to show you that, contrary to what you said a while ago, we haven't got the same sense of humor. (He bows.) At your service."

Franck leaves the room, leaving the novelist pale and dazed, slumped on his bed before the shining computer screen, which is showing in close-up the rape of a little red-headed girl, aged about ten.

15

If hell existed, it would take the form of an ocean
of souls depersonalized by a vain, gigantic collective
movement: you would fancy that sometimes a higher
wave, foaming as it breaks, is a soul illuminated for
an instant by rage and bucking against the torment.

JOSÉPHIN PÉLADAN
THE SORROWFUL HEART

Franck closes the Péladan. His cell phone vibrates, inform-
ing him that the file on Bill Hiscock has arrived. It is
accompanied by a note from Mariella: "But very little about
Ernest Caron. Worked at Brookline Technical College,
1990–2. Taught at Newtonville High School, 1992–2001.
Lives in Boston. That's all." Then a WhatsApp message:

(23:48) Can I ask you something?

(23:50) Of course!

(23:53) I don't really get what's behind this new case. I'm
not being critical, Franck! It's none of my business. It's just I'm having trouble following you.

(23:59) You're probably right. I've no rational or even
emotional reason to pursue it. As I said before: it's

just curiosity. I thought I caught a look, a rather shifty, guilty look. An interesting one. Maybe it was my imagination! But I'm going to follow the trail all the same, and I'm willing to bet whatever you like that Ernest Caron, Le Carré's unhappy cousin, was somehow involved in the murder of the old guy. Anyway, what would I have to do in New York? Rummage in garbage bins? Sort through household trash? No thanks! This isn't a "case." Just consider it a diversion, a whim. But a very important one.

Franck opens the file on Hiscock and reads it through as he leans back, a cigarette between his lips.

Tom Lord was born in 1970, in Pasadena, California. His father held a junior position with the American Chase Bank; his mother was unemployed. They lived in a quiet residential neighborhood. Tom attended a public high school in Pasadena which enjoys quite a good reputation. He was a big, quiet boy, taciturn and a bit dumb. At the age of fourteen, devoured by acne, suffering from bulimia, and spending his recesses by himself, he was suspended by the school principal after a female teacher surprised him rubbing his penis against the belly of a deaf and dumb female student he had cornered in the washroom. He was only allowed to return to school three months later. Now the laughingstock of the school, for the next three years he would be beaten up regularly before finally leaving the establishment. According to him, it was only when he was eighteen, over a shared joint, that he established his first real relationship with another human being, an older boy named Billy Crams. For a year Billy and Tom met every afternoon to smoke grass they bought with the money they stole here and there. They shared their first experiments – first with drugs, then with sex: in 1989 the Pasadena police vice squad opened an inquiry into the rape of Mary Preston, a former classmate of Tom's. Lord was arrested, but Billy managed to escape. A few weeks later he was found dead from an overdose in a Santa Fe motel. Tom was sentenced to six years in prison. Four years later he was out on parole. He worked successively in a record shop, a bakery, a boarding kennel, and lastly a hotel. It was there, in the Winnicot International Hotel, that he met a German producer of porn movies who was attracted by the downcast, dissolute air of the young man and offered him a part. He was required to act out a rape scene "as close to reality as possible" by drawing on his own memories. Initially Tom was a disappointment. Then, chewed out by the producer and humiliated, he threw himself so brutally on the actress – an eighteen-year-old Korean girl – that three actors were needed to prevent him from killing her. This feat of arms gained him quite a reputation in the California porn underground. He made films for another few years, and then ran a fitness club on Hollywood Boulevard. It belonged to the California arm of the millionaire Lance Le Carré. Tom did not meet this businessman until 2009, the year he came to live in a Boston suburb to take over the management of The Muscles of Love, also owned by Le Carré.

The procedure was simple: the cocaine was delivered by some Chechens to a warehouse in Roxbury from where Tom picked it up and stashed it in the fitness club. Then dealers would come to collect it in small quantities. Since 2011 he had been the object of an investigation by the narcotics division of the Boston police, which to date had failed to produce any results.

Among an impressive quantity of notes detailing Lord's daily existence, Franck notices a list of places where he can often be found in the evening: a porn cinema on a service area beside a freeway in Roxboro, a bar on Westwood Avenue, and another bar on Sunbird Street. Franck is struck by one name: the Jaguar Club, on Hammer Street. Then he thinks of Le Carré. Of the models. Of the Special K party. He looks at his watch. It is half past midnight.

Spread over three floors, the Jaguar Club opens its doors to a heterogeneous clientele, from basic suburbanites to the most powerful pimps, from the most fashionable artists to the most talented traders. On the first floor are the dance floor, the stage, the swimming pool, and the main bar. This is where the cards are dealt. This is where all instincts meet. The upper floors are roomier and less noisy. There, intimacy is preferred to the crowd of rutting party animals downstairs. In this way, customers are able to move vertically, discussing business on the third floor, buying dope on the second, and "having a blast" on the first. This kind of arrangement has been popular for the past few years. Private clubs still exist, of course, but Boston yuppies now prefer to go slumming under the aegis of a clinging hooker and warm up in savage style around a chemical bonfire. As for the poorer ones, they look kindly on this raw, inexperienced prey that can't tell talcum powder from coke and don't give the cost a second thought. But what takes place is, more than a business relationship, a genuine encounter. It so happens that people talk to one another as equals, with the more fortunate swallowing their arrogance and the others their distrust. In the Jaguar, different sections of society mingle, different strata intersect, cancel one another out, and are broken down. (It's a real pity, as one journalist pointed out, that such a thing can only happen over a dose of ketamine.)

In general, people are already stoned when they arrive, but they haven't yet reached "the big blow-up," as they call it. The bouncer, a scar-faced African-American colossus, is happy to search customers just for knives and guns. Sometimes he discovers clubs, swords, and even the occasional hand grenade. He turns away the most dangerous or lit-up customers, the ones who have already reached the heart of darkness. Nevertheless, he allows in most of the ones called the "night owls." That is when the shenanigans begin.

The night owls can't wait. They have been dreaming of this all week. Once they are past the Cerberus at the door and the cloakrooms, they rush forward, transitioning from the snow outside to the visceral humidity of the main dance floor. Carried away in their eagerness, they dash, stampede toward the center, flow together. They scream with exhilaration. Some are in tears, half-fainting, while others shriek. The week is behind them. So is work. So is the cold. The hostility of the world and the burden of conscience. Here, all is warmth, light, and decibels. They remain pressed together for as long as possible. This is the rapture of arrival, the euphoria of being isolated from the outside world, of escape. It is the initial deliverance from themselves. It can last an hour, sometimes two. Then they are cast off again – by some change of tack, some aberration by the DJ. But they have to maintain their oblivion. They flow back to the bar, or pop a few pills in the washroom. They bandage their wounds, or inflict new ones. Then they return to the attack, to the conquest of the Unknown. The moment for the "big blow-up" has come. Their arrival had been merely an appetizer, an initial contact, a first step toward collective intoxication. Just a moment of vertigo. The second round is more serious, more violent. They return from the washrooms, eyes popping, nostrils splitting. A glass! They fling themselves forward. They spring. There is a mad rush. A swamp of bodies. They leap, they let loose, everyone is yelling. The music crushes them, grinds them, sifts them. They shout themselves hoarse. They hump one another in their rapture. It's a kind of ecstasy inspired by trifles, one that gathers us, grabs us, shatters, transports us! A magnificent kind of morass that attracts and repels. And we vanish! A magic trick! Smoke and mirrors! Annihilation! All awareness of position, of place, of role. Dissolved! Dancing! To the stars, to the lights, to the DJ's three-day beard, to his face streaked with red tattoos. There is no more inside, or outside. All is flux, reflux, eruption. A cannon spews foam. The participants exult. They drown. They slide on the dance floor, become soapy and shifting. The crowd swells; it stampedes, it riots. There is no more group, nor sky, nor ground, nor self. This is the appropriately named moment of "ecstasy." It is for this that they indulge in such outings. It is on this shining, fleeting moment that they have set their compass. Everything is done, everything is directed toward this moment that the revelers call "blessed." They cling to it for as long as possible. For hours. For the entire night. The heart struggles in its effort... it beats at two, three, four times its normal rate. The DJ, too, is doing his best... the dealers... the barmaids. The magic works, and it lasts... lasts... But, inevitably, the crowd parts. A crack opens. The night owls are uprooted, ejected from the crowd. Brutally cast out, one by one. Thud! on the hard asphalt. Then the final round begins – the longest, the most painful. The most intimate. The collective movement falters, lurches, halts. The tension drops. Awareness returns – and with it the cold and angst. The solid framework of the outside world and the aggressive contours of self-awareness. Faces grow pale. They barely dare look at one another, or look down at the floor, become stable again. Not a word is spoken, not a cry is uttered. Everything becomes unyielding and heavy. Reoccupied bodies go tense. They protest. This is what the night owls call "coming down." They sometimes say, describing this condition, that they are having "the agonies." They had escaped from themselves... Now they are back. They had wished to be outside time, but now they are temporal beings again. Faces are buried in hands. They crack. The entire body almost gives way. Some are still tittering: nerves. Others weep, and wish to die. Others ride it out, rebel: "There's some left? Give it here! Give it here! Hey! Hand it over! A little more? Hey! Just a little?" No, it's morning.

*

Every morning a secretary informs Lance Le Carré of the Jaguar Club's take from the evening before. He smiles, lights a cigarette, and reflects that he doesn't have to worry, for he can invest his hopes in this half-gilded, half-drudging youth: much better than speculating on the stock market. They'll be back the next day. They'll be back every evening. They'll always be eager for a trip, for a break. Le Carré takes a long pull on his cigarette. Anyway, who can forecast the market? Who can say with any certainty where it will be tomorrow, or two days from now? Who can boast of being insulated from a downturn? Le Carré looks at the figures again, and smiles. The Jaguar Club is his harvester, his combine. And the corn is aware of nothing. Of course, some of them actually think they're rebels, a bit Trotskyite. They wave the flag of the Occupy movement, of progressive notions. They see themselves as direct descendants of the great revolutionaries. If needs be, they utter – the next day – extraordinary discourses about overcoming capitalism, oppression, obstacles; they discuss community movements, cooperatives; they provide an opportunity to experience a whiff of resistance. And it's all thoroughly documented! Impeccably studded with quotations! But mostly they're so burnt out they haven't a clue about anything beyond their line of coke.

There is less dancing on the upper floors. There, the cards are dealt differently. People aren't looking for the same thing. The second floor is a checkerboard of small rooms where people come together in groups. They sit at tables, they drink, they snort, they discuss. The ambiance is more favorable to humorous exchanges. Greater sticklers for social differences, more conscious of their own worth, people consume differently, pursue different objectives. It is less a matter of forgetting the self and more of affirming it, less about self-effacement and more about making an impression. Especially appreciated by well-heeled young people (as much for the cost as for the mindset they presume), these rooms provide an opportunity to show themselves off to the best advantage. Fashionable artists, drug wholesalers, and student fraternities have made this their place of choice. The third floor is home to businessmen and industrialists. Come there to relax, they take the opportunity to sign a contract or conclude an agreement. They laugh too, but less unrestrainedly. Their use of drugs is less obvious; they drink discreetly and guard against any behavior that might harm their image. In business there are appropriate times to get drunk (on signing a contract with a Chinese millionaire, for instance), while it would be a gaffe to do so in the company of a member of the gun lobby or a Mormon steelmaker. Here, others are probed, sized up, evaluated. After spending several hours, or sometimes several evenings together, you decide you can confide in your interlocutor, indulge in another bottle, or invite him to share a line of coke in the washroom. Here, people are not trying to disappear – nor indeed to appear. They admire one another, they savor one another. They have nothing to prove, nothing to forget. They are already someone, and are satisfied with their lives.

All these fine folk, gathered into permeable groups, line Lance Le Carré's pockets. Sitting behind his desk, the mobster wears a satisfied expression as he reflects on the Jaguar Club's turbulent nights, in which some shine brightly while others are extinguished. But for him it's always win–win. He loads the dice. He ensures the loyalty of his collaborators. He gobbles them up with their acquiescence! "I play for myself, but they never catch on."

Franck parks the 300C in the club's lot. He finishes his cigarette and gets out. A guy comes toward him, a bearded, tattooed African-American, unsteady on his feet. He takes a few more steps, notices Franck, and, without the latter uttering a word or doing anything, begins to swear at him. Then he collapses and begins to throw up, kneeling on the asphalt. Franck steps carefully around him.

"Asshole!" the individual exclaims, turning toward him.

"Good evening," answers the detective, spinning around and going over to him. "Have we met?"

The man is about to answer, but his body is shaken by a spasm and he begins to vomit again. Then his arms give way, and he falls flat on his belly. Franck goes closer and kicks him in the ribs. Then he grabs him by the collar, lifts him up, and punches him twice before propping him up against the rear fender of a pickup truck. He searches his pockets, finding – in addition to a bundle of receipts, paper clips, and aluminum foil – a small cardboard envelope. Franck opens it and takes out a mother-of-pearl mirror on which he lays the cocaine. The stranger groans, slumped against the wheel of the pickup; he is stained with blood and vomit, and barely conscious. Franck, who has put the mirror down on the hood of the truck, begins to snort. Partway through the line he grunts, and stops. He takes the mirror and smashes it on the ground. Then he takes the pusher by the throat, his gloved fingers gripping him violently.

"You have the gall to sell that crap?" he asks.

The man attempts to say something, but can't. Franck continues, mollified, almost curious, "Do you know I could kill you? Just think about it! First of all, you almost mess up my shoes, then you insult me… And then, to cap it all, you try to poison me!"

The pusher's eyes are beginning to turn upward in their sockets as Franck shoves him against the pickup and lets him sink to the ground. As he tries to recover his breath, Franck goes on, "It would be too much trouble to have to dispose of your body. Get that?"

The guy doesn't react. Then, slowly, he nods.

"Can you speak?"

He nods again.

"Then tell me if a guy called Tom Lord is inside."

No answer.

"Do you want another dose of the same medicine?"

"No… I…"

"Where's Bill Hiscock?"

The man chokes. "Inside."

"Where inside?"

"In a private room… Second floor."

"Thanks a lot."

The nightclub is an inferno, thick with smoke, criss-crossed with green laser beams. A cheap post-industrial torrent – maybe a remix of Wumpscut Sauce Dubstep, thinks Franck – is making the walls vibrate, and a horde of partly stoned night owls seems to be swaying rather than dancing. It smells of sweat and alcohol – and of the frantic obliteration of thought, of self-importance, and of the renunciation of an organic order in favor of a new, mechanistic one. To his right Franck spots a girl of about fifteen sitting on the ground with her head in her hands, her entire body shaken by spasms. Franck remembers his own teenage years. He never went out. He would spend the whole day in his bedroom, surrounded by impoverished factory workers who drank with the same application that they brought to their work, or to procreation. For them, self-destruction was a serious, calculated, precise act. It wasn't debauchery. As for himself, too sickly to pursue a normal school career, he remained stretched out on his bed, drinking tea, and reading when he was strong enough – and, very often, dreaming. The memory of his teen years, together with the sight of this girl, makes him slightly dizzy. Maybe it's boredom, maybe her need to prove something to herself – unless it's just that she wants to "have fun." And why not? After all, it's not her decision, she isn't a rebel. She's simply following the advice of her parents, of friends, of journalists, even of the President: "Just have fun!" So why not her? Why everyone but her? Some people enjoy letting themselves be burned to a crisp on a beach crammed with idiots; others like to prepare vegetarian dishes or carve blocks of ice into animal shapes. She is no more ridiculous and no more to be blamed than they.

Yet Franck still feels uneasy. He looks up. He is dazzled by the strobe lights. Now he realizes what is wrong, what the cause of his distress is. Lyllian must be here, he thinks. He sees the young flutist's smile again, his nervous, diffident gestures, his features. His voice. His drawl. His laugh. And the naivety of his assertion that it is always wrong to kill. Another image materializes, palpable and intolerable: Lyllian snickering along with the models, with a dozen other models who also "just want to have a blast." Who knows if he too isn't sitting on the ground with his head in his hands? In the throes of a spasm? Foaming at the lips? A two hundred and fifty-pound man bumps into Franck, almost spilling his pink vodka over him. A couple of young, sweating transvestites have thrown themselves on the ground and are miming copulation. He feels oppressed, crushed, dejected. Earlier that day, during the Le Carrés' luncheon party, he thought he had discovered someone out of the ordinary. Someone above the basic level. Someone superior to the wretched marshland of ordinary mortals. Someone exceptional, capable of arresting the course of everyday life, of influencing it, of determining his own path through existence. And what a path it was! From the cotton fields to the Boston Philharmonic. What a waste! reflects Franck. Ending up in this place! You can never recover from an evening like this. It's the utter destruction of his dignity. Of his virginity. Give in once and you'll always give in. There is still an icy grip on his heart. He would like to extract Lyllian from this hell. Yes, it's a hell! A cold, stupid, petty hell! Vulgar! Mechanical! He wants to grab him by the shoulders, take him with him, away from this place. Say to him, "Stay there, and don't budge." It's not that he wants to make the flutist his possession. He just wants him not to belong to the models, the pushers, the DJ, the night owls – or to anyone else. They're filth! Franck thinks. Sacrificing every evening on the altar of stupidity and ugliness, wasting themselves in chatter, in trivial escapades, in adulterated dope and desolate sodomy, along with hundreds of other halfwits of the same ilk. A universal dumbing-down, a world of fools who will end by going clean, doing away with themselves, or falling into line. And to think of Lyllian spending his evenings in their company, getting high with them, exposing – and prostituting – himself. These superficial creatures who will eventually settle down, buy the McCarthys' house, the same barbecue, the same doormat. My God! Debasing himself for nothing. Sacrificing virtue without the benefit of vice! Maybe some idiots can emerge unharmed from the foam bath of the Jaguar Club, extract themselves from the horde, go outside, be spewed onto the sidewalk, spend a few days with the shakes, and then go back to what they call "normal life." But, thinks Franck, some scar always remains, some defilement. It's imperceptible to most, but people like me – is there anyone like me? – can decipher the pettiness, the vulgarity, the banality that's left. They'll be like sheep spared temporarily from the slaughterhouse, but still with tags in their ears. They think they're alive, but already they're just hunks of meat.

Franck stumbles to the washrooms. The black guy's powder is burning his throat. Plaster, dammit, plaster and talc. Lyllian's image merges with the dealer's. Sadness gives way to anger. He kicks open the door of a cubicle, evicts the occupant, and bolts the door. Mechanically, he cuts two lines on the lid. I'll strangle them, I'll find them and do them in, he thinks. Franck kneels on the floor, avoiding a pool of urine. Assailed by the smell, by the music, he snorts quickly and stands up. Then he leans back against the cubicle door, closes his eyes, breathing as slowly and normally as he can. After a few seconds he begins to calm down, to regain his composure. His anger fades. His sadness dissipates. The cocaine is reconnecting his thoughts. For God's sake, why did I come out? Is all that any business of mine? We don't even know one another, Lyllian and I! We've had lunch together, but what of it? He stood out against a dreary crowd... How could he not have shone? It means nothing. Gradually, Lyllian's image becomes blurred, more distant. It was just a little fatigue, a moment of weakness, of distraction. And anyway, I didn't come here to look for him, he tells himself.

Franck climbs the staircase to the second floor. The main room is vast, a kind of atrium with small private rooms grouped around it. The smell of alcohol and sweat is still present, but it is airier. The music is not so loud.

It doesn't take him long to find Hiscock. He is in one of the side rooms, sprawled out bare-chested between two brown-skinned women. He is wearing crimson baggy flannel pants and the gilded belt of a Roman centurion. He seems fairly stoned, with a vague look in his eyes, but looks capable of holding a conversation. Franck enters the room and greets everyone. He has recovered his composure and his smile. Hiscock straightens up, masculine and aggressive, his two hookers twittering around him.

"And who do you think you are, asshole?"

Franck doesn't answer. He looks Hiscock straight in the eye. "Mr. Lord, rid me of my suspicion: did you murder, or have murdered, one of your drug mules, a Jimmy Henderson?"

The big man is dumbfounded, but then says, with narrowed eyes, "What kind of crap is this?"

"Did you kill him?"

Hiscock moves a hand toward his pocket. Franck forestalls the movement. He slips onto the edge of the table and with his right foot crushes the privates of the former hardcore porn star. Maintaining the pressure, he asks again, ignoring Hiscock's agonized roars, "Did you kill him?"

"No! No way!"

Franck takes possession of the switchblade and puts it in his own pocket. Then he relaxes the pressure of his foot, stands up, and retreats to the doorway. "I believe you."

The other is still red in the face, foaming with rage. "You'll never get out of here alive! I'm somebody around here!"

Franck, still smiling, raises his voice. "I know who you are, Lord. And let me tell you something: you're the one who's going to get out of here, and fast!"

"Are you—"

"Shut up! The cops will be at your place in Fort Owl any time soon. If you don't want Lance Le Carré to use your balls for a necklace, I advise you to get going. Understood?"

The big guy is dumbfounded. Then he catches on. Without a word, he abandons his women and sets off.

Franck grabs him by an arm, and makes him sit down. "My dear Hiscock, we're not through yet, the two of us. I want to know if Ernest Caron is involved in the business too—"

"Caron? No! What sort of bullshit is this?"

"But you do know him."

"The boss's cousin—"

"You're sure you're not in cahoots?"

"Caron has nothing to do with the business!"

"He knew Henderson?"

"Why would they know one another?"

"Just answer my questions!"

"No—"

Franck brandishes the switchblade. "You're quite sure?"

The fat man swallows, and begins to stammer. "Maybe they've met... But it'd surprise me! I don't know..."

Franck puts the knife away and allows Hiscock to take off at a run. Then he bows and withdraws.

As he is leaving the room, Franck encounters the models, accompanied by Lyllian. The latter, suffering from the effects of ketamine, seems at the same time happy to be alive and on the point of collapse.

"Franck!" he exclaims. "Is it really you?" The models nudge each other.

"Good evening, Lyllian," Franck answers, coldly.

The sight of the young flute player so spaced out, with dilated pupils, doesn't have the effect on Franck that he had feared. His recent fit of sensibility – his "maudlin moment" – is past. He is no longer concerned, just a bit disappointed... disappointed, and weary. Lyllian stumbles and almost falls into his arms, then steadies himself against a wall. Franck doesn't react.

"Say, you look—"

"Yes; I'm a bit on edge."

Lyllian bursts out laughing. The models chuckle.

"But you came all the same! Let's party! There's some shit left over, you know—"

"No thanks."

Lyllian simpers. "Oh, we haven't had a lot, I swear!" He laughs again, and adds, "Listen to this! Stif" – one of the models – "says that one day he injected some straight into his muscles, and his buddies found him on his knees in the kitchen getting it on with his dishwasher! And Tom" – the other model – "got sucked in, literally sucked in by some film or other with Bruce Willis. It wasn't until the credits that he came out of it! Isn't that just too funny?"

"Not really," replies Franck.

"What's the matter?"

"I told you."

Lyllian thinks for a few moments. The models whisper together. "I've got it, Franck!" he exclaims joyfully. "You're judging me! You think it's improper for a young guy like me to get stoned in a place like this! What? Isn't that it?"

"Improper? No. But vulgar."

The virtuoso seems hurt. "I noticed something already, at the Le Carrés'. You like to preach! Anyway, you look just like a clergyman… But, you see, I don't live with Mommy and Daddy anymore. And I don't like people preaching at me."

The models are still chuckling.

"It's not a question of morals, but of purity."

The models howl with laughter. Lyllian is also tittering. "Purity! Franck! You're amazing! You thought I was a virgin?"

"Sensible would have been a start."

"So? It makes you an idiot to have some fun?"

"You have to understand that kind of thing; it can't be explained. As for me, I'm leaving. I'm worn out."

Franck goes downstairs. He makes his way through the mob in its state of fusion. As he leaves the club it is snowing heavily. The sidewalks are white. Two paramedics are busy around a girl having spasms on the pavement. He goes to the 300C. It's better that way, he tells himself. He doesn't feel sad. His affection for Lyllian remained alive as long as he wasn't close at hand. But he has seen his real face: the face of a stupid, naive provincial. The attempt to redeem mankind in general through a singular being always ends in disappointment. It's probably too heavy a load for one pair of shoulders: the person eventually gives way, comes crashing down. So it was with Lyllian. So it was with the others. Faced with universal mediocrity, Franck has sometimes tried to erect the excellence of the particular in opposition to it. But his hopes have always been dashed. So, when he appreciates someone, he prefers to keep well away from that person's physical manifestation and content himself with a memory, a word – or less: a pout of the lips, a glance, the shadow of a nose falling across a cheek. It's less a matter of getting to know the other person than of sculpting a mask and applying it forcefully, unsparingly – and leaving it in place for a long while. That is when admiration, friendship, and love become possible. If the mask falls apart, thinks Franck, it's not only the fantasy that is destroyed: the entire person is demolished. The Jaguar's night owls follow the opposite path. They

119

attempt to merge, to become one, to be consumed in the indefinite – even if it is only for a single evening, a single trip. As for Franck, he tries to deny that part of the other that he has not fashioned himself, the part out of his reach, that escapes him, that exceeds him – the part he cannot control. A loner resists him, pushes him off, tries to forget him (and sometimes succeeds). A misanthrope on the contrary appeals to him endlessly. He needs him. Sometimes he tries to like him. But it is a mistake, for what he desires is the other without his otherness.

The eruptive frenzy of the crazed patrons of the Jaguar Club, as well as the egoism they display during the rest of the week, is a product of contemporary society. Some experts explain this trend by the entry of Western societies into a new phase of capitalism that is less productive, more emotional, more festive. But that explains only the general trend, not the unbridled ferment of recent years. Other specialists put it down to the recent popularity of certain aggressive drugs such as crystal meth or N-bomb. Others attribute it to the colossal success of social networks and their almost daily use by several billion users, and the virtualization of the exchanges that result. In the late nineteenth century several writers deplored – while simultaneously celebrating – a phenomenon of decadence that marked the end of a civilization. Very possibly causes accumulate, or overlap. In any case, Franck tells himself, there can be no doubt that we're coming to the end of something. They, me, Lyllian. Everyone. But this time it may be that nothing new will begin, that the end will just continue to repeat itself. That we'll keep careering farther into the dark.

But, we ask ourselves, why do people choose decadence? It's far from certain that it is in fact a choice. What can the impact of personal choice possibly be? The individual encounters a powerful machine which is beyond him, which transcends him – which destroys his will, fragments it, vaporizes it. Liberalism (in its most aggressive form) posits liberty as a theoretical basis, as a fundamental value, but then goes on to deny it in reality, in practice. Likewise, the use of drugs depends up to a certain point, up to a certain threshold, on the will. But once that threshold is crossed the drug becomes the rule, it transcends the will. Social networks certainly depend on the user's willingness to open an account and use it. But to what extent does the will remain in control? Unless, thinks Franck, the cesspit we are falling into does reflect exactly what we want. And unless our politico-economical framework, far from repressing our desires, actually stimulates and directs them. The night owls of the Jaguar having a blast are fiery, eruptive. The power they enlist to shatter their selves, the passion with which they enrich Le Carré, the way they contain themselves throughout the week so that they can break loose on Saturday nights, all display an incredible expenditure of energy – as well as the intense effort required to channel it.

Franck takes out a Davidoff, slips it between his lips, lights it, and drives off.

16

It is 5:00 a.m. "Strangers in the Night" is coming softly from McCarthy's computer speakers. He leans back in his chair, lit only by the glow from his screen. His features are drawn, concerned. If the Foxtraps offers the sheriff security (and order and meaning at the same time), he is especially apprehensive of these silent hours when the abysses of insanity and alcoholism begin to open up yet again beneath his feet. They devoured his parents. He knows they threaten him as well. My life, he sometimes tells himself, is basically a struggle against my own leaning toward disorder, my own heredity. The drug dealing, the organized crime, are secondary.

The neatly trimmed hedge, the mailbox, and the shiny floor are a valid defense, but there are times when this approach no longer seems adequate – hours of trepidation, perilous hours when he wakens up in a sweat, with everything slipping from his grasp. He looks at his wife – is she still there? Is that really her in that modest nightdress, in this impeccably tidy bedroom? Was it he who painted those watercolors on the wall? He doesn't know. The walls open up; they call to him. "You have no business here," whispers a voice as he struggles, staggering, over to his desk, to his work, curbing his thoughts, controlling himself, warding off all his demons, overcoming them once again, *in extremis.*

The narcs must be about to raid Lord's place, he tells himself. Then he thinks of the whole Henderson case, from old Jim's bloody grimace up to the most recent discoveries in his daybook. The sheriff isn't exactly surprised that his neighbor of thirty years should have been murdered. People tend to think that kind of thing only happens to others, but in his daily activities he doesn't have to deal with distant tragedies. Far from it: the families he rubs shoulders with are caught up in the storm, no longer able to say that that kind of thing only happens to other people. No, what is literally beyond his comprehension is the fact that someone carved up Jimmy's face and made off with his tongue. In police logic, and considering the medical examiner's initial report, that is something scandalous: there had to be two aggressors known to one another but pursuing different ends, or two aggressors unknown to one another, or a single killer with two faces (in other words, two different motives), someone so disturbed that he could savagely cut his victim's throat and then calmly mutilate the corpse. Anyway, in human terms, it makes no sense. It's hopeless, McCarthy tells himself. It means admitting that a person can commit evil for its own sake, with no other motive. You can explain it as the act of someone deranged, of a madman, but madness and sexuality become convenient scapegoats when you have to account for something unspeakable. This perfectly gratuitous act offends McCarthy not only in his humanistic idealism, but also in his conception of the world: it suggests that an act can be meaningless, take place by chance, in disorder. It means admitting that there is a flaw in the machine – a flaw that infallibly points back to himself.

"That's Life" is beginning. McCarthy closes his eyes. He thinks of his wife, his daughters, and his life here at 52 Peacock Street. Together they form a cell of resistance against the outside world. Against cretins who kill, mutilate, and steal tongues. Against the gratuitous. Against delirium. Here, everything is grounded, justified, reasonable. Yet it is no cold construction, ordained by propriety and religion alone. On the contrary: it glows with the love its members feel for one another. But what if this stability is illusory? How long can the family cell resist adversity? How long before it is swept away in the turmoil? Will that turmoil come from within, like the one that swept away the quiet household formed by his parents? Or what if one of those cretins decided to take his revenge, broke into the sheriff's house and went for his wife, his daughters, or himself?

But there is no need to think of such an extreme example, for the nuclear family is at risk every day. Around the dinner table, like yesterday evening, they do indeed make up a family. McCarthy is the father. Charlene the mother. Paola and Anna the children. But once McCarthy goes off to work he is no longer a father: he becomes a sheriff. Once his daughters go to school they become students. What threatens the family, thinks McCarthy, is not so much that gays can marry, not so much that marriage may be viewed as a practical arrangement for settling questions of taxation and inheritance, not so much the way that such half-baked theories spread from universities into the ramifications of daily life. No, the threat is everything that transforms its component parts, making McCarthy a cop instead of a father, Charlene a part-time secretary instead of a loving mother, Paola and her sister future lovers, mothers, and citizens.

As "That's Life" ends, the sheriff has tears in his eyes. He sees a *For Sale* sign on his front lawn. He sees his daughters gone from him. His wife somewhere else, God knows where. Can't we remain together forever? he asks. In the middle of the night, deprived of his family, of his home, he feels the ground give way, begin to shift. So many neighbors, acquaintances, and friends have already been swallowed up... not to mention the ones he picks up every day in the Bellams. Without the order of a stable domestic situation, McCarthy knows he is lost. Many cops have nothing left but their job. It's even a recurrent theme in contemporary detective novels. He, McCarthy, has nothing left but his family. He knows, for instance, that for Jaspers it's not the same. Nor for Hendrix. But in his case he would like his life to be more solid than an illusion, more stable, destined to endure.

As "It Could Happen to You" is beginning, his phone vibrates. Jaspers.

"Good morning, Sheriff."

"Have the narcs finished?"

"The guys searched Hiscock's fitness club and house. All they found was a little powder hidden inside one of those dumbbells that come apart. As for Lord..."

"He got away?"

"He was lying in his garage, dead, with the contents of a submachine gun magazine in his belly."

McCarthy shakes his head. "Anything else?"

"Yes, the narcs want to go over Henderson's truck..."

"We've done that already."

"I know, but they say it was treated as the vehicle of a victim, not of a drug mule."

The sheriff reflects for a few moments. "Tell them we'll do it ourselves and keep them posted."

THIRD DAY

17

When he puts on his uniform, McCarthy forsakes his family; he is no longer a father, but a sheriff. As such, he has to fit into a different set of relationships, admit different unknowns, assume different functions. It is no longer "my wife," "my daughter," no longer Paul, Charlene, Paola, no longer "How was your day?" or "Have you done your homework?" New faces appear: Gomez, Jaspers, Hendrix. An entire universe that he left behind the previous evening re-emerges and takes shape again: the police station, the Ford Cruiser, the murky alleyways, the hostile pimps, an old acquaintance murdered on a street corner, and – God only knows where – a killer who may be preparing to kill again. When he is at home McCarthy tries to set aside any conflict with the outside world, but when he is on the job he is absorbed by it, so he answers his wife sharply when she disturbs him for some trivial reason. "When he's on duty my husband becomes a different man," Charlene sometimes tells her friends, not without some pride. McCarthy himself doesn't see his two sides. He isn't a different man. He is just playing a different part, wearing a different mask – and behind this mask is a sincere, profound actor, who fears a lack of order and a loss of meaning. Whether listening to Sinatra in the squad car with Gomez or on his cheap computer speakers at home, McCarthy confronts the same anguish, the same uncertainties; he obeys the same logic, responds to the same demands. He is a single whole – implying that beneath the sum of his own various manifestations there exists a nucleus that has not yet been shattered. Gomez and Charlene sometimes tease him. They say, "You're a bit of a dork, Sheriff," and "You worry about us so much, honey!" And McCarthy laughs. "You're so precious to me," he tells them. "You make me laugh, and that's something! You love me. And, above all, you help me to know who I am, why I'm alive." Then, in response to this rather pompous little speech, Gomez kids him even more, while Charlene blushes and gives him a hug.

Sitting around McCarthy are Sergeant Wilde, Deputy Gomez, Officer Hendrix, and Doctor Olson. The conference room in the police headquarters is as shabby as the other rooms, and smells stuffy. Apart from Wilde, none of the men present seems to have slept. Hendrix, charged with looking into Laura Henderson's disappearance, is as pale as death, with a black right eye; Gomez, responsible for questioning old Jimmy's few acquaintances, gives the impression he was still working on it until less than an hour ago. As for Olson, he must have gotten drunk to forget the matter of the tongue.

"Where's Jaspers?" asks the sheriff.

"He's completing the search of the pickup with a couple of guys from forensics," replies his deputy.

McCarthy remains silent for a moment.

"First, the important thing is to establish that old Jim was in fact a drug mule—"

"Old Jim?" Wilde interrupts with a hint of irony. "I didn't know you were buddies!"

The sheriff gives him a look. "Sergeant, in Watertown people get to know one another. It's nothing to do with being buddies, it's just a neighborly relationship. Maybe that's something you can't understand."

Wilde is about to justify himself, but McCarthy doesn't give him the opportunity. "Jaspers will contact you soon. If it turns out that Jimmy Henderson did indeed travel for Hiscock, then we'll have a serious line of inquiry, especially now that his employer has just been murdered."

"So you think the two killings are related?"

"I can't exclude it."

"In the meantime, the case has been assigned to the Boston South Police Department..."

"We're collaborating with them. The moment anything comes up to support the hypothesis of a link between the two crimes, we'll take over the entire investigation."

The atmosphere in the room is electric.

"And on our case, what do we have?"

Doctor Olson clears his throat. "For my part, I have to admit there's nothing conclusive, nothing we don't know already. An initial, mortal gash to the throat, delivered by a sharp weapon with a broad, relatively thick blade. Possibly a chef's or butcher's knife... Then the incisions in the cheeks, the eyeballs, and the tongue, using a much finer blade... Not as fine as a scalpel, though."

The sheriff looks up. He asks, "Do we know the time of death?"

"Between five and six in the afternoon."

And to think I was just down the street! thinks the sheriff. There was nothing extraordinary about that in itself. Last year a man stabbed his wife in the police station parking lot when Gomez and Hendrix were on duty. By the time they arrived she was dead. Basically, they were just as ineffective as they would have been if the murder had taken place down some dark alley dozens of miles away. You sometimes hear that a police presence no longer discourages criminals. It's presented as a new phenomenon, and in some respects it is. But there have always been times when a man loses control, is carried away by passion. There may be cops around, a whole army of them... but what difference does it make? The guy lashes out in spite of it.

"Anything else?"

"Just a few trivial details: he didn't have any drugs in his system at the time of death; he had recently eaten a pizza and had breakfasted on a bowl of cornflakes along with a few beers. There were traces of blood on his hands from the piece of venison that was on the seat. No trace of gunpowder."

"In that case, he hadn't been hunting," interrupts Wilde.

"So how do you think it goes, Sergeant?" mocks McCarthy. "You leave home with your rifle and come back two hours later with a nicely wrapped package of meat?"

Wilde isn't disconcerted. "I've never had the opportunity to appreciate the joys of hunting, Sheriff. So I'm counting on you to explain to me what that carcass was doing in his vehicle."

"According to our information, Henderson went to see a hunter friend of his, outside Boston. There he picked up a piece of the venison he'd entrusted to him a few weeks earlier to have cut up and frozen. Anything surprising in that? City folk often do that kind of thing... A whole deer carcass is a bit inconvenient in a tiny apartment. You'll also note that, depending on the species, the law requires two hunters for one animal."

"And this poacher—"

"*Hunter*. He had a permit."

"So you've investigated this... hunter?"

"Gomez paid him a visit. Now, if your curiosity about hunting has been satisfied, I suggest we let the doctor continue—"

"I'm afraid I've nothing else to add."

"Do you know if the CSI people found any fingerprints or traces of DNA?"

"Nothing."

"Thanks," says the sheriff, disappointed.

Next, McCarthy turns toward Hendrix. "What about you?"

"Well, I got hold of Laura Henderson as she was on her way home."

"So she never went to Philadelphia?" asks Wilde.

"She came back. She says Marshall and her had a violent argument on Friday evening, that he came home totally stoned and insulted her. She took offense and hit him, he responded by throwing a plate of soup into her face, and then they smashed up a good deal of the place before she took off for Philly."

"At what time, approximately?" intervenes the sheriff.

"At around ten at night."

"Marshall claims he didn't come home until toward sunrise."

"According to her, he went out again just as she was leaving."

McCarthy and Wilde take notes.

Hendrix continues. "In Philly she went to the place of a friend called Marilynn Bayle. She says she spent the rest of the night there."

"And she came home this morning?"

"Around five, because of her father's death."

"She found out about it in the middle of the night?"

"Yesterday evening, from the newspaper. Marilynn Bayle advised her to spend the night at her place, and that's what she did to start with. Except she says she was overcome by remorse, couldn't sleep, and decided to come home."

"Remorse?"

"For her, there's no doubt that Marshall is the killer… Apparently he confided in her that he meant to 'settle the old guy's hash.'"

"That's pretty explicit," concedes the sheriff.

"So you think it's him?" asks Wilde.

McCarthy throws him a murderous glance. "I've already told you I don't think anything. I'm going to question him again, and we'll see. As for you, Sergeant, do you still think there's a link between our case and the Sherman Valley one?"

Wilde smiles. "Like you, I don't want to rule out anything."

McCarthy gives him a fierce look before turning to Gomez. "And what about you?"

"Nothing substantial. I saw the store where Henderson bought his beer and a few frozen items, met a couple of fat Latinos that he argued with in the laundry, and a clergyman with a goatee that he used to see now and again... There's still the reading group for Western novels—"

Wilde guffaws. "What bullshit is that?"

"I belong to it too," says the sheriff shortly. "I expect your spare-time activities are more honorable, more fashionable, more thrilling. Mine are unpretentious, like Henderson's." He raises his voice. "And now, if you don't mind, I'd like you to keep your mouth shut until this meeting's over."

"You've no right to order me to keep silent."

"I'll answer for it to the DA."

The deputy continues his report. "Nothing there either. Then there was the hunter the sheriff mentioned, a poor bastard who cried a bucket when I got there but couldn't tell me anything except that Jimmy was a good buddy and not much of a hunter."

"That doesn't take us very far."

"I know. But they didn't tell me anything more than what we knew already: that Jimmy wanted to pay to send his granddaughter to a good school. They said it was an obsession of his, that he talked about it all the time. Except that..."

"He didn't have the means."

Gomez nods.

"So he went to work for Hiscock, and started moving drugs."

"Do you think that's reason enough?" interrupts Wilde.

McCarthy turns toward him. "Didn't I ask you to keep your mouth shut, Sergeant?"

"And didn't I answer that you've no right to do that?"

In silence, the two men stare at one another defiantly.

In a voice he is trying to keep calm, but in which the irritation – never mind the anger and contempt – is evident, McCarthy breaks the silence: "Sergeant, it may be that you're not very familiar with what the general population calls 'money problems.' In that case, I'm happy for you."

Wilde doesn't flinch. The sheriff goes on: "You're asking if that's reason enough to begin carrying a little powder across a border now and again? Yes, Wilde, it damn well is. And it's even more so, if you'll allow me to say so, when it's not just your own bread and butter at stake, but someone you love, and this someone is your own granddaughter. Have you read the reports on Henderson?"

"Yes," replies Wilde, icily.

"Then you know that little Julia was the last chance he had to make something of his life, and for that he was ready to traffic drugs, but also, I'm convinced of it, to steal, commit arson, and maybe even kill. You're a winner in life, Wilde, an up-and-comer, so don't be angry! You've a brilliant career ahead of you. But keep in mind that people who have sunk too low in life are capable of doing terrible things, totally crazy things! They're capable of almost anything."

"I see…" answers Wilde, not altogether convinced but being diplomatic.

"What I ask myself is how Henderson managed to get a finger in the pie… I can't imagine him spending time with the gangsters of the Le Carré clan, nor in filthy dives like the Jaguar Club, nor in fitness clubs—"

"Someone might have found out he needed money, and made him a proposition," suggests Gomez.

"Yes… But who was the contact…?"

"Everyone I talked to knew about his money problems… There must have been one or two in the bunch who couldn't have been entirely clean."

"Possibly. But the fitness club is in Fort Owl, and apart from his cousin and a former social assistant, nobody lives out that way."

The door creaks on its hinges, and Jaspers makes a noisy entrance. "Sheriff!"

McCarthy looks at him in amazement. His officer looks distracted, almost panicked.

"What's up? Have you seen a ghost?" McCarthy asks, with a hint of reproach in his voice.

"So what did you find in that truck? Another dead body?" Wilde chips in.

"No…" replies Jaspers.

Wilde raises his arms to the heavens and exclaims, "I knew it! I bet you didn't find a thing! Nobody's finding anything today!"

"That's enough!" shouts the sheriff in a trembling voice, leaping to his feet.

"Are you going to hit me?" asks Wilde, who now seems amused by the whole scene.

"No, but I've asked you to keep quiet!"

Wilde also gets to his feet. "Very well, if that's what you want! I'll note that you are obstructing collaboration between our departments, and blocking my investigation. Now, if you'll allow me, I'll go and dunk a warm croissant in some coffee. All the same, I'm happy to have gotten to know the cream of the police force in this town, who value a fair distribution of wealth and hunting above finding the killer of one of their fellow citizens. Have a nice day." He turns on his heel and leaves through the still half-open door.

McCarthy, Gomez, and the others seem stunned by what has just taken place. Jaspers is first to break the silence. "What should we do?"

"I suggest you answer my question at last!"

"Yes, yes, I'm sorry," Jaspers answers hastily. "Here it is: the two guys from forensics and myself were searching the truck... Well, first I should tell you that my brother-in-law has exactly the same pickup as Henderson... Except it's a more recent model... Naturally, the color isn't—"

"How is that relevant?"

"I'm coming to that, Sheriff! Right, well, my brother-in-law, the other day, after filling the back of the pickup all the way, loaded twenty or so big logs inside the passenger compartment. Then he closed the door, but it was too full and a log shattered the plastic cover on the inside door light."

"And that's what's got you all excited?"

"It's just that, yesterday, when I was searching the vehicle for the first time, I took a look at the lights... I was thinking that" (blushing) "if we didn't find anything, I could maybe take one of the covers for my brother-in-law..."

"I suppose that's not a terrible crime..."

"Well, this is what I'm trying to say: yesterday the cover on the passenger side door was in good shape, and this morning it was cracked."

McCarthy is beginning to understand his officer's agitation.

"So you mean to say that—"

"Yes, Sheriff, somebody must have removed it and put it back again—"

"Between the two searches!"

"He must have forced it a little too much, and—"

"So who can have done that?" asks McCarthy, turning to the others.

"No handyman, obviously," declares Gomez.

"But a cop, that's for sure," says Hendrix.

18

Leaning against the left rear fender of the 300C, Franck has just finished filling the tank. It is sunny and dry; the sidewalks are gleaming. He withdraws the nozzle, screws on the cap, and takes a deep breath of icy winter air and gasoline vapor. Wrapped in his black coat, his features relaxed, he shows no trace of the stormy outbursts of the night before. At the next pump a bearded individual in a fur-lined winter jacket is filling up, while inside the vehicle a woman gnaws hungrily on a chicken thigh. What ferocity! thinks Franck, as scraps of skin and flesh fall to the floor, onto her knees, and between her thighs. They have Quebec plates. They're on their way to Florida for the winter. Most likely own a mobile home they've bought on credit. The woman's fingers and lips gleam with fat. The man has dirty hair and a beer belly. As usual, there'll be lots of fun this year: getting baked on the beach, and cluttering up the Fort Lauderdale old folks' homes and the suburbs of Orlando. He turns away from the couple and goes into the Shell Mini Market.

Inside, a generously endowed blonde named Jenny – she's wearing a name tag – is smiling broadly at a stocky, pimply guy who is insulting her copiously. In a mixture of English and Spanish this individual informs her that she is a fat sow, a fucking cow, and that if it wasn't for her lovely butt cheeks he'd already have made sure she got what she deserved. Jenny, never relinquishing her smile, carefully bags the boor's purchases – a razor, some powdered beef jerky, and a pack of cigarettes. She hands them to him. He responds with a grimace, assuring her once again that she's a stupid bitch, and leaves the shop.

"He's a regular," she explains to Franck.

"Quite a charmer!" he exclaims.

She giggles. "Can I help you?"

"I just filled up at pump number two."

Jenny had been reading the newspaper. Franck can see the headline: *Suspect Denies Being Killer*.

"Oh, still the business about that poor old guy?"

"Yes," answers Jenny. "How horrible!"

"Exactly how horrible do you find it?"

"Pardon?"

"What I mean to say is what would you be prepared to do to the killer if you got your hands on him?"

She blushes, but her smile doesn't fade. "Well... I... I suppose I'd call the police and—"

"You wouldn't kill him?"

"Oh, no!"

"Really? But after all, he mutilated his victim!"

Embarrassed, Jenny looks at her cash register, then at Franck, and then back at the cash register before asking, "Will that be all?"

Out of the corner of an eye, Franck notices the Quebecker, who has entered the shop and made a beeline for the frozen food section.

"No, I'd also like a booklet of matches, please."

The Quebecker, pretending to examine the plastic trays of lasagna he is holding in his right hand, uses his left to spirit away several packages of frozen foods. Jenny seems to have noticed the maneuver too. She continues smiling nevertheless.

"That comes to $48.86, please."

Franck takes out a fifty-dollar bill and hands it to her, then picks up his change and starts to leave. But he stops in the doorway, eager to witness the outcome of the little scene being played out inside the shop.

"Pump number one," announces the Quebecker.

"Will that be all?" asks the girl at the till.

"Yes."

"Aren't you taking the frozen peas as well?" she asks.

"What frozen peas?" answers the Quebecker in a flat voice.

"The ones you have under your coat," she says, still smiling.

He reluctantly puts them down on the counter, pays for his gas, and goes out at the same time as Franck, who gives him a long look that contains a hint of awe.

"What are you gawping at?" asks the man in the winter coat.

"Nothing at all! I just find you—"

"You find me what?"

"Extraordinary!" exclaims Franck. "I've rubbed shoulders with neurotic millionaires, cunning mobsters, and psychopathic murderers. I've personally turned over a half-ton of garbage! I've stuck my nose into some bloody, juicy cases... And I'm something of an odd bird myself. Yet you're my first frozen-pea thief!"

"I'm not going to stand—"

"I'm sorry, but the best part of all is that you didn't turn a hair! Someone else, anyone, would have tried to justify himself, protested he hadn't meant to, would have dashed outside, or produced his knife. But not you!"

From the pickup the woman is observing the scene with a gloomy expression. Finally she lowers the window and asks, "Is there a problem, Gary?"

"No, honeybun!"

"Honeybun!" exclaims Franck. "He calls her honeybun!" He roars with laughter.

The Quebecker turns around, caught off balance. "Why don't you just fuck off?"

"I'm sorry! But I'm feeling in a rare good humor. And it's partly thanks to you!"

The Quebecker doesn't reply. He hurries toward his pickup, gets in, and drives away.

Franck, back in the 300C, calls his secretary. She answers after a few rings.

"Good morning, Franck!"

"Mariella!"

"Well, you seem in excellent form!"

"You're perfectly right!"

"The Boston air?"

"The Boston air almost killed me."

"So, what explains such excessive good humor?"

Franck starts to drive off. "I just met a very siliconed Barbie and a frozen-pea thief."

"A frozen-pea thief?"

"Frozen. That's what I said!"

She seems to reflect for a moment. Franck is now driving along Crescent Street.

"But that wasn't the reason why you called, right?"

"Let's say it wasn't the only reason…"

"Go on, then."

"I'd like you to make an appointment for me with the principal of Watertown High School."

"Where Ernest Caron used to teach?"

"The very place."

"When?"

"Today."

19

There is something intolerably barbaric about visiting museums.

MAURICE BLANCHOT
L'AMITIÉ

Parked in the lot of Boston's Museum of Fine Arts, Franck cuts a long line of cocaine on the back cover of *The Supreme Vice*. He snorts noisily, swallows, and wipes around his nostrils with his handkerchief. The speakers of the 300C are playing "Agnus Dei" from Fauré's *Requiem*, recorded by Michel Corboz with the Bern Symphony Orchestra. Franck lights a cigarette, closes his eyes, and smiles. He feels the warmth of the sun on his face. What a lovely day! he thinks. Bliss depends on very little: sunshine, the right amount of cocaine, and a frozen-pea thief. So basic! Childish, almost. But here I am, carrying on like a therapist! A personal development trainer! How awful! Why not write a book about it? So much stupidity! But even stupidity is splendid this morning—

Someone knocks on the car window. He opens his eyes. An obese, mustachioed security guard. "Even stupidity is splendid," Franck repeats out loud with conviction, and laughs.

He lowers the window. "What can I do for you, officer?" he beams.

"I'm sorry sir, but there's no smoking on the museum precinct."

"Not even in my car?"

The guard nods. "Not as long as it's in the museum parking lot…"

Franck takes a puff, stubs out his cigarette in the ashtray, and the guard leaves.

Mankind may be ugly, and pitiful, but there's no denying that there's something comical about it! Franck savors a simultaneous appreciation of simplicity and the picturesque. Aware that he himself will never be caught stealing from a deep freeze, and that he will never wear the uniform of a museum guard (or carry the three hundred pounds of unhealthy fat that go with it), he locates his wonderment in the distance that separates him from such curious individuals, the way an intellectual waxes enthusiastic about the simple way of life of a primitive tribe, even envying them a little – though without wanting for a moment to be like them. What only a few hours ago he would have considered the acme of vulgarity now has the same effect on him as an elegant pirouette – man compensates for the misery of his condition by a perpetual burlesque, by a hearty roar of laughter. Except that they're quite unaware of the spectacle they are providing, thinks Franck. Often they don't even applaud one another! Far from it; they hate one another, suck one another's blood!

But this reservation doesn't prevent him from concluding, as the "Libera Me" is ending, Why should I care? It's a lovely day! And the rest of it will be lovely too!

Electrified by the sunlight, the drug, and the pea thief, Franck bounces rather than walks into the main foyer of the Museum of Fine Arts. This institution opened its doors in 1876, and has been in its present location since 1909. It is one of the great art museums in the United States, with several dozen galleries and more than 450,000 works. Noted for its large collection of Impressionist and Postimpressionist paintings, the building also houses hundreds of Greco-Roman relics, a considerable quantity of Carolingian jewelry, illuminated manuscripts, and, of course an impressive range of painting and sculpture from the modern and contemporary periods. Franck's last memory of it dates from about ten years ago. At the time he visited the complex room by room. He had haphazardly devoured hundreds or thousands of works, from high antiquity to the most daring contemporary art. But the whole thing had left him cold. The paintings and sculptures ran into one another. It became merely an agreeable overview of human genius, nothing more. Since then, Franck has not visited any museums – or at least none of those great souks devoted to the fine arts which are above all a display of pride, though what they offer our admiration is not so much the works or the artists, but the city or country. It gives me infinitely more pleasure to look at a reproduction, Franck thinks. And art books have the advantage that you can consult them whenever you feel like it, outside opening hours, in the middle of the night, and on your own – thank God, on your own! Free of the heterogeneous conglomeration of tourists that park themselves in front of you, exclaiming, sneering, or incriminating, free of the ecstatic yells of tour guides from midday to four, free of the blasé or belligerent gaze of the guards, and finally free of the excess that telescopes six thousand paintings into one, leaving you only with a grotesque feeling of stupefaction.

But in spite of all this, there is something agreeable about the sight of hundreds of tourists swarming into the entrance hall, and Franck, leaning against a classical-style column, savors the spectacle of the new arrivals who, depending on their mood (and culture), are bellowing, roaring with laughter, or photographing one another.

Oh! Look at her! That big fat woman! Wouldn't she make you weep with joy! German, or Swedish maybe! In her canary yellow dress, chirruping away! But no husband in sight... He'll have sobered up after his night on the town and, hey presto, he's hanging himself from a light fixture. As the cocaine takes effect, Franck feels a desire to go up to some tourist or other and tap him on the shoulder, introduce himself, and initiate a discussion – but he has no idea what they could talk about.

Van Gogh, Gauguin, and Cézanne have a place of honor in this Bostonian pantheon of the fine arts. The gifted Post-impressionist trio have individual rooms devoted to them, and their names in gold on the plaque are enough to excite the tourists, who rush to be immortalized by standing next to it (and then go on to do endlessly likewise before Van Gogh's and Cézanne's self-portraits or Gauguin's *Where Do*

We Come From?). Some seem to be there only because of a hastily drawn cross in their guidebook, others because an acquaintance back home had advised them to spend at least an hour or two in the museum, and others to see some work they have heard praised to the skies since they were children; some have actually come out of genuine interest. Franck notices a group of students gazing around them as they trot along with a thrilled expression, armed with notebooks, ballpoint pens, and smartphones loaded with the app put out by the museum; a group of young adolescents led by a hysterical teacher braying out information about the artists loudly enough to be heard all over the gallery; an old woman on the verge of fainting, so moved is she at the prospect of finally seeing Monet "for real"; and a couple of overweight, erudite Americans who maintain to whoever wants to listen that the French and Italians would be better off reviving their economies instead of making sketches. Yet here and there a young man or young woman is sincerely moved. "Ah, now there's a wonder!" exclaims Franck, as a female hunchbacked dwarf in an artificial leather miniskirt enters the gallery. "What a glorious variety of human beings! What abundance! I'll see a few thousand like that in the day! And all of them seemingly so different, but all so fundamentally ordinary!"

Fiddling with the brochure handed him by an attendant at the information desk, Franck wonders which paintings he will look at. A few are enough. Once you cross the critical threshold of a certain number of works, art becomes a fool's game, a social diversion, an obligatory genuflection before human genius. Just like going to bed with two, three, or four partners is fun, but beyond that consumption wins out over sensation, and it becomes just a big meat market. For the same reason, a conversation with ten or fifteen participants is seldom of any interest: numbers kill personality (and in a place like the Jaguar Club that annihilation is at a maximum).

Although some amateurs stubbornly overlook the fact, a work of art always comes garbed in its own legend. This may be rooted in nostalgia for a certain period (the effervescence of the 1910s in France or in Austria, for instance), in a political event (the advent of Francoism in the case of *Guernica*), or in certain outstanding events in the life of an artist (Van Gogh cutting off his ear) – unless it simply consists in the prestige it acquires by belonging to the "art world" and by being hung in a famous institution. So a lot of visitors go around clutching a plan with a finger firmly on Van Gogh's or Picasso's name, falling into raptures only when they are absolutely sure that the merest sketch they have before them was drawn by the same hand that painted *Starry Night* or *Les Demoiselles d'Avignon*. They aren't being dishonest, just expressing their respect for history, culture, and the institution. It is also quite possible to appreciate a period without liking the works produced by its artists. The enthusiasm and abundant production of artists in the 1910s and 1920s are striking, but never, good Lord never, has a single goddam canvas by Mondrian or Léger managed to elicit the slightest tremor of emotion from me, or awaken my interest, thinks Franck. People rarely look at a painting for its own sake. That can only happen at certain moments, in certain circumstances. Unfortunately, it's very difficult for those special moments to be accommodated by opening hours, long lines awaiting admission, and the bacchanalian surfeit typical of major galleries. Once we have sincerely contemplated a half-dozen works we usually keep going borne along solely by our fascination for the notion of Art – or perhaps simply by the thought that we have paid the full shot for our ticket.

"You're looking thoughtful, Franck!"

Franck turns around and smiles at Lyllian. "And you're late!"

They shake hands.

"My dear Lyllian, you seem strangely in form after the night you've just spent! Can it be the famous privilege of youth?"

The flutist laughs. "Maybe, Franck. You too, by the way! Last night you seemed… a little tired. And I still have no idea what brought you to that club!"

"Yes," answers Franck, maintaining the lighthearted tone. "I behaved badly toward you, and I hope you'll forgive me."

"But no—"

"I'm serious! What I said to you did have some truth, though it was exaggerated, overdramatized. But my tone was inappropriate. My behavior wasn't horrible, but… I was lecturing! Yes! You called it preaching; I call it sermonizing. There's nothing worse. In my defense, I'd barely slept, I was overcome by angst, and I'd snorted too much coke. In addition, I'd got my hands on a musclebound rapist who confirmed my suspicions—"

"Your suspicions?"

"Yes!" (Franck winks.) "I think I've cleared something up…"

"Related to what?"

"I can't say any more for now. But maybe a little light has been cast on the mystery behind the murder of that old drunk that the press is having such a field day with—"

Lyllian is startled. "Franck! Really?"

"Yes, but that's not so important. What really matters is that you be convinced that my apology is sincere."

"Maybe we should call the police and—"

"Am I forgiven? I'd understand completely if you still bore me a grudge… After all, I didn't show myself in a very good light. Will you let me try to justify myself? But maybe I'd just be adding to my uncouth behavior…"

Lyllian, taken by surprise, doesn't answer.

"Well, you see, I have an ideal: purity. But it's a holdover from a different age – no, I'm sorry, all ideals are holdovers from a different age! I just want to say that it's a nocturnal ideal, an anguished ideal that signifies nothing more than the neuroses of whoever professes it. The other evening, when I was so hard on you, I was spaced out, fraught with the absolute. How could you have understood me? After all, you're not an angel, just a little bargain-basement succubus, if you'll allow me!" (He laughs.) "If I'd been in my right mind I wouldn't have expected anything of you that was beyond your ability. It's just that I got carried away… And my angst won out over my manners. I was alone, in that vulgar nightclub, where people descend to the level of beasts, of machines. And there I was, saying to myself, 'Lyllian is here! Among them, with them! He's not here to collar a murderer, nor for the pleasure of observing like a naturalist, nor to mock, criticize, or despise, no, he's here to enjoy himself! He's making common cause with these people! He's one of them!' At that moment I hated you. Disappointment can make you more acerbic! You weren't doing anything wrong, but it was worse: you were doing the same as everyone else. And instead of toning it down – for I went tone-deaf (ha ha) – and asking myself, 'Franck, what are you doing?' (But right then I was no longer sure my name was Franck.) 'Why don't you just leave him alone? Come on! He's no worse than the next man: far from it (he's more elegant)! He's a young man like a thousand others. And he's from Texas! From Texas! Of course that's a handicap... But he's not doing so badly... He plays the flute! Maybe that's the source of your disappointment! – an artist, what a stroke of luck! But what's a flute player? A fool full of wind. A windbag with a purpose, basically. Don't hold it against him! Go instead and wish him good evening, enjoy yourself, and leave him in peace.' But instead of saying that to you, I lambasted you, made you my whipping boy, and buried you under my psychopath preacher's – no, sermonizer's! – raving."

Lyllian is stunned. He frowns, trying to understand. Finally, he stammers, "If I understood you properly... you despise me..."

"More than anything, I'm asking for forgiveness," Franck protests.

"Yet you—"

"Now, now!" Franck answers with a laugh. "The greatest philanthropists only become so out of contempt. If people were strong, if they were great, what excuse could they find for them?"

Lyllian, eager to bring this conversation to an end, answers, "Don't worry, Franck, I forgive you willingly."

"Oh!" cries the detective with tears in his eyes. "Thank you!"

"I'd just like to add that I have a guilty conscience toward you too … It was really a bad time for us to meet."

"It's nothing! Anyway, we didn't come to the Museum of Fine Arts to act out a soap opera. Where do you think we should begin?"

"What would you say to Manet?"

Before heading up to the level where the Manets are exhibited, the two men pass through the security check. A huge, ruddy-faced guard scrutinizes visitors, searches the occasional bag, and pats down a few men. "Anything dangerous in your possession?"

"Anything dangerous?" Franck repeats.

"Any blunt instruments, anything with a cutting edge, inflammable liquids?"

"No, just a machine gun," he answers with a smile.

The guard laughs and waves them through.

The Manet gallery is vast, and sober. Well, thinks Franck, at least they didn't have the bad taste to do it up in nineteenth-century style!

The Parisian painter's pictures are spaced out, well-lit, without an excess of documentation. The visitors, although they are relatively numerous, are considerate enough to whisper and not exclaim too noisily when they spot the

Olympia or *Le Déjeuner sur l'herbe* (except for one fat Dutch or Flemish lady who is a frequent visitor to museums and wants everyone in the room to know it).

"Do you know Manet?" asks the flute player.

"Just to see!"

"Manet was born into a family belonging to the wealthy French bourgeoisie: he had everything he needed to become a somebody, a notary. But he chose painting, and scandal along with it. It happened almost in spite of himself. The poor man wanted to be a respectable painter, the glory of the Salons. But he made a false step with his *Olympia*" – Lyllian points to the painting – "and he was launched into a bohemian existence, punctuated with scandals and brandished walking sticks."

"That's very well put!"

"Do you know this painting?" (He is still pointing at the *Olympia.*)

"I do, but by name only!"

"Well, it's one of the very first paintings of modernity, hailed as it deserved by Baudelaire, whom we both admire."

They come to a halt in front of the painting.

"Look. For us, at first sight nothing seems especially shocking. But put yourself in the context of the time: a woman, almost a girl, not just nude, but truly *naked*, devoid of any of the usual mythological trimmings. You're not looking at a goddess; no, this girl is a prostitute. And underage, into the bargain! And the cat...!"

"Yes, that does ring a bell..."

"That cat was at least half the cause of the scandal. Contrary to what Zola thought, or pretended to think, it could only have served to underscore the sexual connotation of the work. I ask you, what can this cat possibly represent but the vagina the girl is covering with her hand?"

"That's really fascinating," declares Franck, though he is no longer smiling and is feeling a bit drained.

They move on to *Argenteuil.*

"It looks Impressionist."

"You couldn't be more right! But it's the work of a different kind of Impressionist, as Manet wanted to keep his distance from the movement. He was chosen as its master without wanting it. This painting represents a kind of encouragement to his followers, to Monet's 'gang'. It was a splendid way to do them justice."

Franck looks at the canvas without any great conviction.

"Come, Franck. Here's *Le Déjeuner sur l'herbe.* What can I tell you about it?"

"I'm sure something will occur to you…"

"Well, the young boy in the center is said to be the illegitimate son of the painter – who, between us, was quite a womanizer. It's really something, isn't it? Have you noticed the lovely treatment of the light?"

They move along, with Lyllian chattering on as he moves confidently from one painting to the next, recounting the history behind each, describing its context, slipping in a few anecdotes, a few technical details, or recalling the historic scandals they provoked when first exhibited.

Some visitors, attracted by the youth of this extemporaneous guide (a change from the aged ones usually on offer), have begun to follow him; they shower him with compliments and keep close at his heels. By the time they reach *A Bar at the Folies-Bergère* it has become a real procession.

"Ah! Just look at this! This is his masterpiece!"

"Another one?" asks Franck.

"No, no, his *true* masterpiece! His absolute masterpiece! In comparison with this, the others are just appetizers!"

Franck nods.

"Just look at the supple execution! The shimmering light (Velázquez was the only master he recognized)! He was near the end of his life when he painted what I consider a kind of testament." He raises his voice. "Can't you sense the approach of death in this play of mirrors exalting appearances, the ephemeral, the fragility of existence?"

Before they leave the room, Lyllian receives a salvo of thanks and congratulations. "You'll go far, young man," predicts an English lady who resembles the late Queen Mother in her dress and hairdo. A financier from Seattle insists on embracing him, while the man's wife religiously takes down his contact information. The flute player smiles and clucks, pressing the hands that reach out to him. "You're welcome! Only too happy!" The ovation continues for another few minutes, and then the two men leave the room.

Lyllian seems delighted. "Did you enjoy the tour?" he asks.

"A lot! Now I know for sure that you're cut out to be an actor."

"Really? What makes you think so?"

"The baloney you were spouting, of course! It so happens I've already read it word for word. In some booklet, I think… Some Taschen art book, perhaps. But what does that matter? You didn't utter a single heartfelt or personal word. Not one risky idea. Nothing to show who you are… It was just parroting! All an act!"

Lyllian turns crimson. "Franck, that's not true!"

Franck laughs, and slaps the flutist on the back.

"Come on! You know perfectly well I'm right. You read some brochure while you're sitting on the john, and then reel it off to everyone you bring here – and they swallow it, the idiots; they're your audience. As for you, you're an adorable actor. Full of someone else's words, you perform marvels. Obviously you have to renounce your own identity, to compromise. But what does that matter? You'll go far! The prospect of an excited public will direct your fingers much better than any conductor could. You'd commit murder in order to please. So would I! But here's the thing: not to please others! You see the difference? You're just like that little tart in the Manet painting."

"Stop!" cries Lyllian.

"Oh, come on! I've drunk your watered-down wine without complaint. I think that deserves some consideration!"

"You're mistaken about me!"

For a few moments Franck says nothing. They go down the staircase.

In the main hall, as Lyllian is about to leave, the detective catches him gently by the arm. "Listen, I'm not going to apologize again."

They stare at one another. Then the flute player looks away. "I'm going. Goodbye."

"As you wish, Lyllian."

The flutist goes down a few steps, then turns and cries again, "You're wrong!"

Lyllian heads for the exit, but then stops and makes for the washrooms.

"Now I'm presentable again!" exclaims Franck, after combing his hair and examining himself carefully in the mirror. He unscrews the silencer from the Steyr TMP and slips it into his pocket; he returns the pistol to its holster and then snorts a short line of cocaine from the back of his cell phone. Then he carefully closes the door of a cubicle where the flutist lies in a pool of his own blood, his torso riddled with bullets.

Now that's what you call drawing a line under a friendship, he smiles to himself. Then he leaves the washroom, whistling the "Libera Me."

In the entrance hall the swarm of visitors is thicker than ever. You'd think it was *La Musique aux Tuileries*! My flutist would probably have had something very profound to say about that! thinks Franck as he threads his way through the motley crowd of wonderstruck tourists; he notices a big blond guy pretending to sodomize a Greek statue, an Asian taking a selfie between two mummies, and a French mother out of her mind because she has "lost Anouck! Anouck! Where's Anouck?" – but then she finds Anouck behind a fluted column and bursts out laughing.

Reaching the door at the top of the monumental staircase that leads outside, Franck feels a shiver run through him. (And I didn't even see the Van Goghs! he thinks.) He hesitates for a few moments. Then, making up his mind, he makes for the parking lot. Sitting in the 300C with the Fauré *Requiem* just coming to an end, he consults his messages.

Mariella: "Appointment Patricia Froger school principal 4:30." He enters the school's address in the GPS and then, checking that the guard is nowhere near, lights a cigarette.

After all, he reflects, my little Texan windbag wasn't so awful... It was just that he was itching to play to the gallery. He'd have killed for a few whistles... The appeal of the crowd, of the stage, of that brief instant when all eyes are on you – when, for a few moments, you're bigger, more solid, the only thing that exists – is probably what motivates the neophyte artist. But Franck judges the flute player severely in comparison with the men he admires: gifted artists, now long dead. He knows them only through their biographies. He can't understand how such books can have been written by admirers who make every effort to introduce "inner necessity" as a smokescreen to obscure the constant, aggressive trait of vanity. Lyllian, in his desire to please, was no more repulsive than the bulk of visual artists and daubers, or the sludge of pianists, dancers, and carvers of PVC. He was no more stupid than any novelist, thinks Franck. He actually had that rather cold elegance lacking in most American artists, as badly dressed as they are stupidly optimistic. The fact is, I had no reason to wish him harm. Closing his eyes, Franck takes a prolonged drag on his cigarette, then exhales a substantial cloud of smoke.

"Maybe I was a little hard on him," he repeats to himself. Then, opening his eyes again, he drives off.

20

Handcuffed and sitting on a metal chair, Alexander Marshall spits on the floor and declares categorically, almost solemnly, "I ain't sayin' nothin' more." Then he straightens up, and his face closes. He has adopted the pose of cool insubordination, the defiance of a convict, that brutal assertion of the will which – in contrast with the inevitability of the conviction – generally inspires more pity than respect. Beside him, his lawyer puts away the documents spread on the table in a file folder, and then confirms, "My client won't be making any further statement."

McCarthy nods. "Return the suspect to his cell," he orders two officers who have been following the interrogation from an adjoining room, behind a one-way mirror. Then he says goodbye to the lawyer and leaves the room.

In the next room, Gomez is sitting with a large mug of coffee in front of him.

"Did you hear everything?" asks the sheriff.

"No," answers the deputy. "I came in at the end."

McCarthy sits down. "He says he didn't know Hiscock, but he's lying. I know he's lying."

"Because of Laura Henderson?"

"Because of her, and his computer."

"What did she say?"

"That Marshall and Hiscock met on at least two occasions."

"At their place?"

McCarthy nods.

But even without Laura Henderson, even without Hiscock's contact information found on Marshall's computer, hidden under the borrowed name of a household appliance store, McCarthy would have bet that the two men were acquainted – though less on account of any strictly logical reason than because of a certain similarity, a family likeness. Those two are a perfect match, thinks the sheriff. And indeed they share the same rocky itinerary, the same need to dominate, the same appearance of fate.

"So," asks Gomez, "could it have been Marshall that introduced Hiscock to old Jim?"

McCarthy reflects for a few moments. "I think it was Laura that mentioned Hiscock to her father. That she was the intermediary." McCarthy stops, and then goes on. "Maybe I'm a bleeding heart, but I like to think that Laura actually wanted to do something for her daughter, just a gesture… No big deal! Just lift a finger! The hope that there was still a glimmer in her, a hint of goodness that…"

"That made her hope that young Julia could make it in life."

McCarthy nods, then asks, smiling, "Do you think I'm being naive?"

"No, Sheriff, I think that if reality can really be dark, human beings" – he mechanically touches the gold chain of his crucifix – "are still capable of earning themselves a few bright spots… rare though they may be."

"Thanks," answers the sheriff.

McCarthy's gratitude is sincere. In response to the cynicism that is common in some police departments, and which is mistaken for realism, the sheriff and his deputy try to approach humanity from its least repugnant side. Sometimes they simply aren't able to, or else the thread they are grasping at frays through. Yet they go on hoping. Their effort is as much a moral as a professional obligation. "If everyone is as wicked as they say," they sometimes repeat, "what's the use of getting up every morning? What's the use of risking your life, and your family's? No, if we do get out of bed it's because there's some hope, a glimmer that guides us when we put on our uniforms in the middle of the night, buckle our belts, and pick up our guns."

"So, Marshall brings Hiscock to Laura Henderson's…"

"Then she introduces her father as a potential drug mule…"

"He still has to agree."

"His daughter convinces him. He loves little Julia, so he accepts."

The two policemen fall silent. Each is reflecting inwardly.

It isn't all that rare for a man who has gone straight all his life to embark on a criminal career in later years. Often he is simply driven to it by the financial problems resulting from the inadequacy of his pension. Such is clearly Jimmy Henderson's case. But it can also be interpreted as the sign of a last-minute rebellion against a social order that has crushed him for forty or fifty years, exploiting him while forcing him to grin and bear it, robbing him while expecting him to express gratitude. So, when he reaches retirement, he rebels. He starts to frequent underage hookers, or push crack. In Canada, a 101-year-old grandmother got caught putting heroin in her cup of coffee. When the cops arrived, she just looked at them with a mischievous little smile that said, I've come to an age when you can't touch me. I've seen it all! Now it's my turn. I can give you the finger the way I've been given it all my life.

Gomez breaks the silence. "So you think Hiscock is mixed up in our case?"

"That seems plausible... But to what extent? Was he directly involved in Henderson's death? It may be just a coincidence... On the one hand there's Henderson's murder and the mutilation of his corpse, and on the other there's Hiscock and the stolen drugs. There are logical connections between the two, but no clear cause and effect."

It is the absence of any tangible line of inquiry that frustrates the sheriff. There is no clue, nothing coherent. Just an ordinary guy found on a street corner in unusual circumstances. Around that, vague explanations, but nothing adequate. Suspicions, but no corroborating facts. It may have been a settling of scores, as often happens between drug traffickers; it may also have been committed by Alexander Marshall, but – and this is McCarthy's thinking – there may be a third angle...

"You see, Gomez, we've explored the Marshall angle and the Hiscock angle, wondering what links there might be between them. But it's possible we've gotten it all wrong, that this murder was carried out by a killer who wasn't acting in any rational way, or was following some code we don't recognize, a genuine lunatic we know nothing about except that he's roaming our streets – and that he's a killer. A guy acting without any motive apart from his own pleasure."

That is what frightens the sheriff. Basically, there is nothing surprising about a totally crazy crack addict murdering his own father-in-law, nor would there be anything unusual about the father-in-law being murdered by his employers because he was dabbling in drug dealing on his own account. You can talk rationally about these two examples; maybe they are justified by the statistics. The citizen with his head in the newspaper just gives a sad shrug: that sort of thing is inevitable. It's also possible to situate them geographically: in the Bellams, a deprived Boston neighborhood where countless sordid events occur, or at Fort Owl, in a shady fitness club run by a former porn star. You can reconstitute an itinerary, suggest explanations, and sometimes even justifications. Human beings are always human. But what can you make of a crime the only motivation for which is the pleasure of committing it? How many people would be capable of murder for a reason like that? Very few, McCarthy would like to reply. But he's not convinced. Maybe that kind of crime usually just remains unsolved. When a gang leader is found dead with a dozen bullets of different calibers in his body it's easy to get your hands on whoever's responsible: you just have to look at the competition. When a rich dowager has been butchered in her mansion and her jewelry taken, there's an explanation, and very often only a little persistence is needed to uncover the precise circumstances. But when one guy stabs another in the open street, without any motive apart from a desire to exercise his power, where is the investigator supposed to begin? He can't form even the vaguest impression of a killer like that, for he can look like anyone. He doesn't necessarily live in the Bellams or in Dorchester; he doesn't necessarily haunt the murky streets of the periphery, where the trafficking goes on, where gangs are organized, where clever robberies and villainous crimes are planned; he hasn't necessarily gone from prison cell to prison cell. Maybe he lives in a big house in the center of Watertown, in a henhouse deep in Hidden Hills, or, as often happens, in an ordinary home in a law-abiding neighborhood, apparently leading a law-abiding existence. The sonofabitch could live in the Foxtraps, on my street, be my neighbor, McCarthy thinks.

This final thought turns the sheriff's blood to ice. He thinks of his daughters. Of his wife. If he's certain his family has no connection with thugs like Hiscock or Marshall, there's nothing to say that they don't encounter a killer every day who, in the anonymity of a family backyard, is preparing to commit some massacre. So, in God's name, what can I do? How can I protect them? he thinks. His nocturnal angst grips his heart again. It's no longer merely the unpleasant prospect that their investigation may lead nowhere, that justice will never be done. It is the immediate, chilling perception of danger, his impression that the threat may come from any direction – and that there is nothing he can do about it. Nothing, except spend his days with his family, armed, waiting for the bastard to turn up. But is it possible for such a man, who is capable of murdering another human being without any apparent reason, to live comfortably in one of the comfortable homes in the

Foxtraps? Is it possible for him to live an ordinary life, to attend neighborhood parties, to take his kids away for the weekend, to clip his hedge, to cook on the barbecue? Does he have the same white mailbox, with his name on it, a completely ordinary name? My God, he thinks, shouldn't his name at least be written in capitals? Is it really possible for him to go unnoticed? But most likely he can, and McCarthy knows it. He distrusts depictions in terms of good and evil, of struggles between angels, with explosions, an enormous din, celestial drumbeats, cries of glory, and gorings. That kind of hyperbole leads to the fanciful nicknames that the press bestows on murderers: The Vampire of Düsseldorf, the Milwaukee Cannibal, the Butcher of Rostov... beasts, monsters, and demons all. If people tried to be a little less sensationalist, he thinks, we'd have some nice surprises: The Electrician of Amstetten, The Insurance Man of Orlando, The Accountant of Thunder Bay. Who's to say Gomez and I aren't dealing with the Potter of Watertown?

The theory of a psychopathic killer is taking shape; Hiscock and Marshall fade into the background. Of course, other possibilities remain – and there can't be any question of releasing Marshall or refusing to clear up the Hiscock murder. But at this precise moment that isn't what McCarthy believes: Marshall is too obvious, too predictable. He could kill, and maybe he did, but he didn't commit this particular murder, he's sure of it. "It could just as easily be you or me, Gomez. Someone who's around but nobody notices, someone no one has noticed."

The deputy nods.

"Unless this isn't his first... Hendrix has been looking for similar cases. The only plausible profile is that of a certain John Doyle, jailed for three murders – old women whose throats he cut before he disfigured them with the help of chemicals. But right now he's still inside... Apart from him the psychiatric services have suggested a few names, a few angles, but nothing substantial."

"Let them keep looking."

And if we find nothing, what then? thinks McCarthy. Will the killer strike again? Has he left town? Is he still among us? And above all, for heaven's sake, what kind of a guy can he be?

21

Spacious, well lit, and tastefully furnished, Patricia Froger's office is in striking contrast to the remainder of the building, which is austere and shabby. Sitting in a white leather armchair, the principal of Watertown High School wears an icy smile that betrays no hint of emotion. Her tone is courteous, dry, and precise. She is taking no pleasure in this interview. But as the principal of a highly reputable establishment it is appropriate for her to speak to a private detective – as long as there is nothing reprehensible about his investigation and it does not involve one of the students.

"So," continues Franck, "Professor Ernest Caron quit entirely of his own accord?"

"That's what I said."

"Did you make any effort to keep him on?"

"No. As I told you, he was a serious, trustworthy employee, well-liked by the students. But he had made up his mind to leave."

"From one day to the next?"

The principal hesitates. "I... I think he had come into an inheritance, or something like that."

Franck smiles. He glances quickly at Ernest Caron's file, which is open before him and which includes his written resignation. "May I read it?"

The principal sighs.

The detective reads the document. Then he returns it to the file, closes it, and smiles broadly.

"Mrs. Froger, just one more question... How much did Lance Le Carré pay you for your silence?"

Startled, she blushes. "I beg your pardon?"

Franck slides the file slowly toward the principal. He is still smiling. After a moment's silence he asks, almost in a whisper, "What were your specific reasons for *firing* Professor Ernest Caron?"

22

As soon as he was warned that the premises of one of his men were about to be searched – and that the man in question was suspected of involvement in the widely publicized murder of a Watertown retiree – Lance Le Carré had immediately done the necessary to get rid of him, so that Hiscock never reached his apartment. The gangster then made certain that his contact in the Watertown Police Detective Unit was taking care that any trace of drugs in old Jimmy's vehicle would disappear. Hiscock is not the first of his employees he has disposed of; likewise, he has corrupted more than one public servant. Such things are, so to speak, merely an aspect of normal business. But Le Carré is feeling uneasy about the encounter between Hiscock and Franck, which has been reported to him by one of the two tarts. What was this guy doing at the Jaguar anyway? he wonders. How is he mixed up in this business? And what does Ernest have to do with it?

A few weeks earlier, on the recommendation of a friend, Le Carré had hired Franck to carry out a tricky operation. It consisted in recovering some important data from a Canadian mafia don. Le Carré's own men couldn't be involved. Le Carré had contacted Franck. The two had met briefly, then he'd had no further news from the detective until two days later, when Franck called him from Ontario. Le Carré had invited him into his home. He had paid him. So what's the guy still doing here? That's something Le Carré can't figure out... Accustomed to viewing human relations in terms of profit and loss, he can't understand why an employee he has already paid off is still on his territory. It makes no sense. None of his other bagmen behave like that. He gives orders, they carry them out; he pays, and they disappear. So why doesn't this one do the same?

Le Carré lights a cigar and then dials Franck's number. Franck responds on the second ring. The gangster puffs on his cigar. He waits for a few moments, ejects the smoke, and asks in a calm voice, "Are you trying to double-cross me?"

"No."

"Who are you working for?"

"I'm working independently."

"In that case, tell me why you're tracking *my* men right into *my* nightclubs, to investigate *my* family? Who are you working for?"

"I repeat, I'm working independently, Mr. Le Carré."

"So it's for yourself you're attempting to connect Caron to the death of some old waster?"

"You remind me of my secretary!" exclaims Franck. "And, if I may inquire, why do you attend fashionable exhibitions in Boston? Well? I'll tell you why: it's because you like to. Well, it's the same for me: I'm investigating your cousin on a whim, just because I like to!"

Le Carré doesn't understand anything of this. He's being taken for a fool! Angrily, he stubs out his cigar in the marble ashtray, and declares, "He's not the killer."

"I never said he was."

"He had nothing to do with that murder!"

"He'll have an opportunity to deny it."

The gangster covers the mouthpiece with his palm, and calls to one of his men in a low voice, "He's going to Caron's! 77 Francis Street. Bring him back to me." Then, to Franck, "There won't be time for that." He hangs up.

Furious, Le Carré gets up. He paces up and down in his office. Is Ernest capable of something like that? He's an odd fish, all right. But kill someone? He considers that the beatings, kidnappings, and murders he pays for belong to the rational sphere. They are financially justifiable. Very often their only purpose is to protect him from competition, to preserve an advantage, to maintain his profit margin; they are required by necessity, by circumstances – what Le Carré calls "fate"; they are the result of planning, of foresight. The principles underlying his crimes are identical with those observed by any business leader with minimal ambition. But what's the sense of leaving this old guy mutilated on a street corner? It defies logic, and he hopes the guilty person will receive an exemplary sentence.

But what if the bastard really is his cousin? Hasn't Caron always been odd? Didn't he have to intervene personally a few years ago with the school where he taught after the parents of a female student discovered a worrisome correspondence between their daughter and her physics teacher? (Caron had written "I'd like to slip my tongue into your skull after I've boiled it" to the teenager.)

But that's just stuff you write, thinks Le Carré; it doesn't mean anything. My cousin's no lunatic.

23

"For the individual lacking in high resolve and unable to react against the tide of the times, the general decay of ideas and concepts leads to a formidable phenomenon of enticement." Reclining on Ernest Caron's sofa, Franck is reading aloud from *The Supreme Vice.* Three cigarettes have been enough to give the professor's tiny living room the appearance of an aquarium. *"The sapping of willpower that is accepted, the pairings that debase the scholar ruled by his cook, the poet by his daughter, the husband by the wife; all this pusillanimity has an aim, namely the huge relief of abdicating all agency, the nirvana of passivism, total indifference to the dignity of life, the definitive collapse of human respect: in a word, a hypocritical pretext desired by the cowardly to allow them to declare that they bear no responsibility."*

The detective interrupts his reading, lays his book on the coffee table, and on it cuts two lines of coke that he snorts slowly, then throws his head back and closes his eyes.

No. 77 Francis Street is at the extreme edge of Watertown, a stone's throw from Mount Auburn Cemetery, in one of those dead-end neighborhoods of which there are thousands throughout the country. The roadway is potholed and the houses are poorly maintained, with weeds growing up to the windows. It's not that the people living there are poor; they just don't care. Ernest Caron doesn't care either. His Mercury, parked in front of the house, is rust-eaten and the hubcaps are missing; the windshield is cracked, while through it can be seen an accumulation of fast-food wrappers, old newspapers, and parking tickets. The path to the door is overgrown; the massive, robust front door has been tagged by neighborhood pranksters; the entrance hall is narrow and dark, lit only by an ancient light fixture surmounted by a flower-patterned shade that casts just a feeble glow; there is a lingering odor of incense, mothballs, and stale meat; the kitchen is cluttered with the normal bachelor's mess; the tiny sitting room where Franck is sitting is encumbered with aged furniture, the wallpaper is yellowing, and the bookshelves hold a jumble of scientific books, periodicals, the MIT monthly newsletter, and a modest collection of jazz CDs. Franck has laid his machine pistol on the low wooden coffee table.

"*Frailty of the will is of all ages. The decadent, a broken marionette with strings hanging loose, lacks even the resources needed to relocate his vice and move to a different midden; he rots where he is, content with this irritant which, in exchange for the few rights it takes away, also removes all duties. Contemptuous of his liberty, which is a burden to him, he longs for the tyranny of a vice. In the age of chivalry one held one's own life cheap; in ages of dandyism one holds one's own freedom cheap.*"

Franck sits up, folds over a corner of the page, and lays his book on the table beside the Steyr TMP. Then he looks Professor Caron straight in the eye. "Have you calmed down?"

The carrot-top, gagged and handcuffed to his chair, answers with a nod.

"I'm delighted."

Franck goes across and unties the gag.

In the sheriff's office, Laura Henderson is sitting across from Gomez and McCarthy.

"Thank you for coming, Ms. Henderson," the sheriff begins.

She nods, looking pale.

"You are here as a witness, of your own free will."

She nods again.

"Do you still maintain that Alexander Marshall killed your father?"

She shrugs. "Who else could it be?"

Gomez leans forward. "Why not some drug trafficker your father was working for? Maybe he met someone at your place. Bill Hiscock, for example?"

Laura shakes her head. "It was Alexander, I tell you. Hiscock had nothing to do with it."

Professor Caron stares at a point on the yellow wallpaper in his sitting room.

"Have you swallowed your tongue?" asks the detective.

Caron doesn't answer.

Franck takes a pull on his cigarette. He spews out the smoke, and after a moment's pause asks, "And old Henderson's tongue, what did you do with that?"

The professor's eyes widen. He shivers.

"You're afraid to look at me?"

No answer.

"You're afraid to look men in the eye, isn't that it, Professor? You've been made fun of, despised, endlessly pushed aside, you've never been granted a glance of desire. Isn't that so? The eye, which they say is 'the window of the soul,' has never been anything for you but a tepid orifice through which all kinds of filth is dumped on you. So, old Jimmy Henderson—"

"Be quiet!"

"Come on! I know very well you didn't kill him."

Caron nods, as if this was obvious. "I was following you..." he finally gets out.

"But I shook you off."

"Yes... But then I saw you in the distance, as you were turning onto Parker Street, where—"

"Where you stumbled upon a corpse. And you indulged in your bit of meddling. Did your bit of surgery: the tongue. Added your personal touch!"

"Stop! You don't understand at all!"

"Understand why you slashed a dead man's eyes and then stole his tongue? Of course I understand. You prefer the company of the dead to that of the living. I haven't come here to blame you!"

"I know why you're here," declares the redhead in a somber voice.

Franck shrugs. "Go on."

Caron hangs his head, resigned. "You're here to get rid of the only witness to your... Well, you... You're here to kill me."

*

Gomez and McCarthy are puzzled. "How can you be so sure?"

"I know him." That is enough for her. She knows his past, she has seen him at work, waiting for her daughter to step out of the shower, beating up kids suffering from withdrawal. His need to dominate, the beatings she got, and even his way of knuckling under to Hiscock and thugs stronger than himself. It all adds up to a killer's profile. The sketch may not be precise, but it's clear enough. "That guy killed my father." For Laura there's no room for doubt.

Gomez speaks more softly. "Did he say anything to you?"

"He told me to keep my mouth shut."

"About what?"

She shrugs. "He was always telling me to keep my mouth shut."

The sheriff takes over. "Have you any concrete reasons for thinking he's the killer?"

Laura smiles. "You want to see my bruises, Sheriff?"

He sighs. "No, it's your father's wounds that interest me—"

Gomez intervenes. "Was there any blood on your partner's clothes?"

She thinks for a few moments. "No," she finally says. "I didn't notice anything."

Franck lights another cigarette. "Do you smoke?" he asks Caron, holding out his packet of Davidoffs.

The other man swallows with difficulty. "No."

"You should. It's relaxing." Then he flings himself backward on the sofa. It's really depressing in this place, he thinks. And he feels a certain sympathy for Professor Caron rising up within him. Can anyone live like this? Here? With this furniture, my God! This wallpaper! The smell… This conventional collection of CDs… The daily humiliation of never meaning anything to anyone. Nothing, ever. Caron could die and lie here rotting for a year before his mobster cousin would – maybe – send someone to check on him. It all began when he was a teenager. It always starts in adolescence. Until then, on the whole, you look no different than the other kids, and there's always a doting grandmother to show you affection. But then you grow older, get acne, become ugly – and you simply cut yourself off. You used to be a "strange kid," now you're a "solitary young man," "a bit mental." That's okay for some… They accept the role naturally. But others cast blame, they resist. They approach the herd, awkwardly. They stammer, they blush, they drip sweat. They have imploring eyes. They're crazy for acceptance. But the herd doesn't want any part of them: it bleats, it pushes them away; they have to retreat to the barbed-wire fence in the farthest corner of the pen. It goes on like that for several years. Then a few swallow their humiliation and manage to join the herd. They drop out of school. Find a job. Have more or less normal relations with their coworkers. Unless of course they go to university and manage to shine in some student society. Sometimes they find themselves a wife and have kids. They "found a family," as they say. But then there are the others. They never manage to escape from their exile, or adapt to it; they're crazy for human contact, for women, for everything they've never had. That's Caron. Franck feels tears welling up in his eyes.

Suddenly he sits up and stubs out his cigarette on the table. Then he gets to his feet and throws himself on the physics professor, pulls him to him, envelops him completely in his arms. "Poor man," he murmurs in his ear. "Poor, dear man." Weeping, he kneels in front of him. He takes his hand and kisses it. He recognizes all the distance that separates Caron from someone like Lyllian, or other artists he has met. They aren't outsiders; they're outstanding. The public, while sometimes perplexed by them, embraces them. They're free to keep their distance from it, to reject it, despise it. They always find it ready to welcome them back. But people like Caron lack that security. Theirs isn't an "alternative lifestyle." For them, there's no alternative.

Regaining his composure, he backs away as rapidly as he had approached, and returns to his place on the sofa. He lights another cigarette.

"Your impressions will be taken into account, Ms. Henderson. But we didn't bring you here to talk about Alexander Marshall." After a pause, Gomez goes on. "You're here because you agreed to collaborate with us."

She sighs, and then says resignedly, "Go on."

"What can you tell us about the... unsavory relations of your father with drug traffickers?"

Laura starts. "Not again! You're going in circles, Sheriff! I told you they had nothing to do with it. You're obsessed by—"

"And you," interrupts the sheriff, "who are you obsessed by? Who are you protecting?"

"I don't understand—"

"Hiscock was your lover?"

Laura pulls herself up. "What gave you that idea? You're crazy!"

Franck looks the carrot-top up and down. There is a glint of amusement in his eyes.

"So apparently you think I've come to kill you?"

Terrorized, the professor nods.

"Because you're... a witness?" adds Franck.

"Yes."

"And what did you witness, pray tell?"

"Henderson's murder, of course!"

"What?!" exclaims Franck. "You think I killed the old guy?" He roars with laughter.

Caron is dumbfounded. "But... I was following you... It's true... I lost you, but then—"

"There! You lost me! You've said so yourself. And when I left Henderson after greeting him, he was very much alive."

"Then why are you here?" asks Caron.

Franck clears his throat. "I'm just playing a game, my friend. It's just a little diversion for me. I'm so bored in New York, in Boston, everywhere... So, when I saw you the other day, sunk down in your chair, crushed by your family, dragging your history, your sackful of saucepans, your personal cannonball! Crushed! I said to myself, 'Now there's a strange guy.' But most of all it was your eyes. When we talked about the old guy's murder you trembled, and there was a gleam in your eyes. Do you know what that look expressed? A secret. Yes, a little secret that has kept me entertained for more than a whole day. I came here to confirm my intuition."

Caron doesn't understand. This individual, obviously on drugs, maybe as mad as a hatter, who has broken into his home holding an automatic weapon, doesn't fit any of the categories he usually uses to judge his fellow men. What kind of person tracks someone down just for his own amusement, for the sake of no more than a little entertainment? No, no, he's lying to me. He did kill the old man. He knows I know. He's here to finish the job, he thinks.

"I don't believe you. You were the killer and… you're going to kill again."

"You're obsessed! And what makes you think, tell me, that I'm this fearsome ogre?"

"My cousin hired you, didn't he?"

"So that means I must be a killer, right? And that's why you followed me the other day, isn't that so? A killer, a real one, one that fascinates you, excites you! You, so morbid! So impotent! You, the half-man! Someone who takes his fury to the limit, for whom it isn't enough to cut pieces off old dead guys, who can look someone else in the eye without blushing, without flinching. You think I'm that kind of man. And you idolize me."

Caron starts to protest.

"But I'm not that man," Franck continues, his tone suddenly uncertain. "No, my friend, you're wrong. I'm no killer. Until today I'd never killed anyone. Yes, I confess. I killed that young flute player who spoke so badly about Manet."

"Lyllian? But why?"

"Who knows? Did I really want to? Did he irritate me?

Maybe it was just for the pleasure of making a pun about drawing a line under a friendship? Maybe I only acted on a whim, out of desire for a fresh sensation? For me, everything's so boring, so worn out. I try new things... But I'm already tired of killing, I admit it."

The redhead is perplexed. "I don't understand at all..." He raises his voice. "Who are you, anyway?"

Franck considers the question at length. Then he lays out a line of coke on the table and snorts it before answering, "I'd like to be able to tell you something original. But I have the impression" (a veil of sadness comes over his eyes) "that I'm just a marionette, a rickety kind of nutcracker doll. Or worse, a fictional character that the author is trying to motivate with the most flagrant contempt for the rules of human psychology. A perverse author with a thirst for freedom, for fantasy – but who can't do without fate, without the banal. I seem crazy to you... but I'm not; I'm just an ordinary little addict that any doctor could explain completely. You find me colorful, brilliant... wrong! That's just a knee-jerk reaction to a drab world. You think I'm self-confident: well, maybe you're braver than I am! You asked me who I am... What can I say? A mask – that's what I am. A mask imposed somehow or other onto something shattered, that's slipping, slipping. Glue doesn't stick very well to nothing!" He gets unsteadily to his feet. "So ask yourself whether I deserve to have you for a fan club, with your damfool morbid little embellishments. I'm simply in the process of dying."

As Franck is preparing to leave, the professor calls to him: "You... You haven't told me... If you didn't kill old Henderson, then who was it?"

Franck shrugs. "Who do you think it could be but that drug-sodden thief they arrested a few hours after the murder?"

"Alexander Marshall?"

"Most likely!"

Caron is uneasy, almost scared. "Then…"

Franck's tone is serious, lugubrious. "Then things are exactly as they seem."

He leaves.

On Francis Street, in front of Caron's house, a number of vehicles are parked. They're returning to the fold, thinks Franck. In kitchens, in living rooms, bachelors are pouring themselves a beer and families are mimicking happiness – the ambiance of a residential neighborhood at dusk. Franck gets into the 300C. He looks in his rearview mirror. Behind him, the black van hasn't moved. Inside it, Le Carré's two enforcers, hastily dispatched to capture Franck, are still bound and gagged. He lights a cigarette and drives away.

24

In the Ford squad car, Gomez and McCarthy are sitting in silence. Sinatra, too, is silent.

"Yes, Laura Henderson was right: I was crazy. Crazy to think that Hiscock had anything to do with the murder. Crazy out of arrogance. Crazily fanciful. Crazy for complications. It was all under our noses. It was under our noses all the time." The sheriff has been repeating this since Jaspers burst into his office to announce that it was all over: "Marshall has just confessed."

Marshall had confessed. And then nothing more, just a buzz. He said where the weapon was. They found it. The DA has been informed. The press too. "Well done guys, you did great work." The popping of flashbulbs, hands being shaken, hugs: a little glory. And that was all. Night has fallen. The police station has emptied. Everyone has gone home. Case closed. Only McCarthy and Gomez linger on.

"So, is that it, then?" asks the deputy.

"That's it," answers the sheriff.

And this evening already the headlines will roll: SUSPECT CONFESSES; HE WAS THE KILLER; BELLAMS DRUG DEALER CHARGED WITH MURDER.

A case like that wouldn't provide the plot for a block-buster. The residents of Watertown will shrug as they drink their coffee, as if to say, "I told you so."

"My instinct! Like hell!" growls the sheriff. "More a lot of bullshit, that's what! It's just that I wanted to make a mystery of it, to silence the voice that was telling me that basically it had to be him." The sheriff sighs. He adds, "I was hoping for a discordant note."

More silence. Then Gomez speaks. "The good side of it is that it makes it easier for us to do our work... Take the young woman you find lying stiff in her kitchen, well, nine times out of ten all you have to do is talk to her boyfriend; he's probably come home wasted and beaten the crap out of her, that's all. The movies are all the poorer, but we—"

"We lose out too," grumbles the sheriff. "Not as cops, not as moviegoers, but as human beings. Isn't that so?"

Gomez doesn't answer. He presses Play: "It Had to Be You."

"Want me to drop you at home?" asks the deputy after a few moments.

"No, not at my place. I want to... reflect." (He gives a weak smile.) "I want to be a cop for a little longer... Drop me at Captain Carl's."

"Any objection to some company?"

Captain Carl's is an ordinary pub on Buffalo Street, patronized above all by family men who linger on after work, reluctant to slip back just yet into cozy habits, and in addition a few of the usual losers, and a few harmless crackpots.

"Good evening," says McCarthy in a flat voice as he enters.

"Two heroes!" exclaims big Tommy, the pub's owner. He comes out from behind the counter and literally throws himself on the sheriff, flinging his arms around him.

"You've heard the news already?" says the deputy, surprised. Tommy taps his BlackBerry with a knowing look.

"The press didn't waste any time," sighs Gomez.

"Neither did you!" exclaims the barkeep. "Congratulations! You saw right away who you were dealing with. In no time at all! A few hours and he was in the slammer. And I heard that—"

"Bring us a couple of beers."

Tommy nods and goes off to fetch them.

"I can see we're going to spend the week explaining that we didn't do anything out of the ordinary," says the deputy.

"I'm soon going to have to explain that to Charlene and the kids." He can already imagine his wife hanging on his neck, hugging him, and whispering in his ear that she went out to get "a big pie and a bottle of wine," as his two daughters shout their joy. Among the series of misapprehensions that await the sheriff, this will be the most painful. For him, the rowdy admiration his family shows him is a trial more than a source of gratification. He sees it as a misunderstanding, the commencement of a lie.

"Are you okay, Sheriff? You're very pale."

McCarthy tries to smile. "I'm thinking, that's all. After these days of craziness – or absence of craziness, if you prefer, it's quite normal…"

As silence is about to fall again, Gomez risks a question that still bothers him. "But Sheriff, didn't Doctor Olson's report suggest there might have been two killers involved?"

McCarthy nods. "As of now, Marshall hasn't said anything. We'll question him again. What do you expect me to say? Maybe he was carrying more than one weapon... Now that he's started talking I'll make sure he doesn't keep anything from us."

McCarthy raises his beer glass. So does Gomez. Glumly, they clink glasses.

"Another round, Tommy."

Gomez left an hour ago. The sheriff feels no desire to go home. He is comfortable here, with guys who, like himself, aren't ready to go home. He recognizes Pasteur, the gas pump attendant who waved to him as he came in. He saw him laboriously searching his pockets for change, and – hesitatingly, guiltily – scraping together enough for a beer. Pasteur is a drunk of the lowliest variety – the kind that don't have enough money to pay for their vice. He'll pay for a second beer, then borrow from other customers. Then he'll plead with the barkeep to grant him some credit before he sets off for home, whining and dissatisfied, made vicious by his residual thirst, ready to pick a fight with anyone. Then there's little Griffith, who once had dreams but swapped them long ago for a job as a city employee and a lease on a German car. And Samson, a former neighbor the sheriff had lost sight of for a few years. And McGaffey, whom he arrested for dealing cannabis five years ago, but who doesn't seem to hold it against him. Finally, Tarpist, a mustachioed seven-foot colossus, who was thrown out by his wife after she found more than four hundred videos on his computer depicting nude, leather-gloved, cigarette-smoking women. And then there's me, he thinks, just as reluctant to leave here as those guys, just as loath to reflect, and who has just ordered another beer. He sighs. Yet I need to reflect, at least to convince myself that the whole thing isn't a farce, McCarthy adds to himself.

When Tommy sets his beer down on the table, the sheriff looks at him curiously, thinking, Now there's a guy who'd never have allowed himself to get carried away, who'd never have allowed his imagination to get the better of him. If I'd consulted him from the start, he'd have told me without a moment's hesitation that Marshall was the guilty one. He's not obliged to deal exclusively with people who are depraved, in crisis, driven by impulse. He knows them in their ordinariness.

"Thanks, Tommy!"

"You're welcome, Sheriff. The next one's on me!"

As McCarthy is taking his first gulp, Linda comes into the bar. With garish makeup, liberally sprinkled with perfume, atrociously bloated, and dull-eyed, she greets the drinkers, who look away. The only people she frequents are on the Internet. She met them on a "conspiracy website," shortly after 9/11. She happened on a site explaining that the official version of the events was questionable. She posted a comment. Someone responded. Then she became convinced that the things she heard on television were untrue. She was completely won over by the theory

of an inside job, which claimed that the Bush adminis-
tration was behind the attack. Within a few weeks she
was radicalized. By the time a member of the forum
came for a visit, Linda was convinced that George Bush
was conniving with an extraterrestrial brigade. After fifteen minutes, her visitor, a handsome electrician from
Dorchester, a widower who organized bingo games to
raise money for the blind, received a dummy call on his
cell phone saying he had to deal with an emergency and
made his escape. The business about extraterrestrials was
too much for him. Ten years later, when she was leading
a solitary existence and had gone partly crazy, the Edward
Snowden affair burst on the scene. From that moment
on, Linda was no longer alone. There was no one at
home with her, no one around her, no one to answer
her messages, but she did have the company of the US
government, spying on her, listening to her, taking an
interest in her.

Tactfully, Tommy goes up to her, greets her, asks
for her news, and requests (indulgently, as if talking to
a child) that she not bother the other customers. Big
Linda protests, declaring that she just wants people's
attention for five minutes – it won't take long – to talk
about an earthquake deliberately provoked by the CIA,
the Illuminati, and an extraterrestrial brigade. Tommy
shakes his head. "I'm sorry, Linda. You'll have to do
that outside. But if you promise me you won't cause a
disturbance, I can serve you a beer." Open-mouthed,
torn between her convictions and her thirst, Linda
hesitates. Then she looks up, and says, "Okay, I'm
going."

Good old Linda! thinks McCarthy. She may be nuts, but there's something attractive about her. She can rage, recriminate, be dead set against the whole world, but she'd never harm a fly. Basically, she does her best.

McCarthy doesn't much believe in the big – fantastic, Hollywood-style – oppositions between Good and Evil. In the abstract, they make sense, he thinks. But on a human level you find them all mixed up, interwoven, overlapping. And then, who is *good*? Who is *evil*? Most people are neither one nor the other; they are at the mercy of uncontrollable circumstances that govern their lives. So they do something, and then the politicians, the clergymen, and the cops come along and slice up what they've done, categorizing each piece as "good" or "bad." The sheriff remembers a religious fanatic who worked on the police switchboard and was found partly responsible for a death after she implored a 911 caller to "not even mention such horrors," and hung up on them. It was out of goodness, of course – a goodness that gave a psychopath from the Bellams time to saw up his girlfriend with no interference, despite three desperate calls to the police department. Maybe I'd be better off if I just didn't give a damn... He sighs, and sips his beer.

"You don't seem quite yourself, Sheriff," Tommy intervenes. "Upset about that sonofabitch?"

McCarthy nods. "I was sure it wasn't him... How dumb can you be!"

"I have to tell you that as soon as I read the newspaper I said to myself, 'That's the one!'"

"That's what's upsetting me..."

"Anyway, you were right to keep looking. I just tell myself that that guy's a murderer and it's obvious... But he mightn't have been *your* murderer."

McCarthy gives a bitter laugh. "Yes, that's what my job comes down to: matching the right murder to the right killer."

25

He told himself that sin penetrates the deepest intimacy, that it binds two people together no less than the most burning caresses, that private, intimate, shameful transgression makes us penetrate the existence of another as deeply as the carnal act makes us penetrate their body.

WITOLD GOMBROWICZ
PORNOGRAPHY

The bar is almost empty. McCarthy is starting on his third beer.

"Good evening, Paul."

He looks up. The man is wearing a violet-colored velvet jacket. He recognizes him. "Franck!" he exclaims, in a slightly slurred voice. "I never thought I'd see you again! What are you doing here?"

"I came in to see you."

The sheriff is astonished, almost wary. "Really? And how did you—"

"I saw you from the street. It doesn't look as if you want to leave this place…"

"That's right, Franck! That's right! You've read me perfectly…"

"Because of your wife?"

"Oh come on, what must you be thinking?" He gives a nervous laugh. "Everything's fine with my wife."

"And with your daughters too, I know. Yet you've no wish to join them, not this evening."

The sheriff smiles. "Right again," he confesses, bitterly.

Franck leans toward McCarthy, and whispers, "Would you like to know what brought me in here, Sheriff? It was just that – the fact that you don't want to go home."

"I beg your pardon!?" McCarthy exclaims.

"May I sit down?"

The policeman nods.

Franck sits down, and continues, "Reality has played a dirty trick on you, Paul. You were on the track of an unusual killer, some bloodthirsty, scintillating guy, an ogre, a fairy-tale character! And then – oops! – with a bounce of his shoulder he knocks you up against the hard truth, against the Bellams, against the obvious, against Alexander Marshall. It would take less than that to drive you out of your mind…"

The sheriff doesn't reply. He shivers.

Franck goes on: "The obvious, Paul… It was all obvious. All as expected. Predictable. Banal. Your life is banal too. Nothing ever happens in it, except what must. You know Charlene is expecting you, that she's bought a pie, that she's dressed up for the occasion. Your poor little house is ready to welcome you – your castle that protects you, but suffocates you too. You're afraid of losing your grip, Paul, and you feel, in spite of everything, that with this case you've crossed a line—"

"I'm going home very soon."

"If you keep on drinking," Franck goes on, "their surprise will turn to uneasiness. That's why you're here, why you're lingering on… Isn't that so? To undo the web you've spun… To enjoy a little lightheadedness."

Franck covers the sheriff's hand with his. McCarthy's face clouds over. "And you – what has brought you here?"

The detective smiles. He leans in close. "You need an ally, Paul."

26

As soon as you construct a fictional universe that
has the false extremes of bourgeois mediocrity and
pathological eccentricity as its two poles, the style
that imposes itself automatically is a contorted one.

GEORG LUKÁCS
THE PRESENT SIGNIFICANCE OF CRITICAL REALISM

Suite 478 in the Grand Conference Hotel is immersed in
semidarkness. The curtains are drawn. A strong, complex,
noxious odor – a mixture of Casablanca lily, wallflower,
and turpentine – pervades the room. McCarthy is rooted
to his chair, motionless, his eyes closed. Before him, on a
side table, in the shadows, sits the dirty china which just an
hour before held braised breast of Bresse pigeon, fillets of
gilthead bream, mullet with Espelette peppers, veal sweet-
breads, saddle of lamb Prince Orloff, and a Madagascar
vanilla-flavored *biscuit soufflé.* On the table are two empty
glasses and three bottles of Saint-Estèphe; little scraps of
aluminum foil and a silver spoon reflect the (feeble) light
cast by three massive candelabras.

The metallic voice resumes its psalmody: "*Bianca seemed
the very young daughter of this recumbent Venus, who, with las-
civious satiation, displayed the animal seduction of her potently
voluptuous body to the gallery.*"

McCarthy is emerging from his torpor. He opens his eyes. Franck, standing on the bed, naked, his back arched, violently, extravagantly, is holding the Péladan volume at arm's length. The flames from the candelabras cast a glow over his face and body. His lips are red, his eyelids painted with garish eyeshadow; his hair seems darker, while his ravaged features, with dark circles and prominent cheekbones, have a corpselike pallor. His eyes express a hard, cold determination. He falls silent for a moment, holding quite still. The sheriff is suddenly overcome by anguish, by pangs of withdrawal. He senses that the spectacle cannot end here. That it must continue. That there would be a kind of false note if it were interrupted at this point in the text – at this juncture in the feast. He clenches his fists. Tenses up. He starts to get to his feet, to open his mouth, to speak. But suddenly, to the policeman's relief, Franck, with a sway of his hips, steps to the left. He passes one hand behind his back, puffs out his chest, arches his back even further, and resumes his recitation.

"*She already possessed her full figure, her warm complexion; her bosom was a woman's and her hips held a promise of fertility. A prayer-book angel, denuded as a foolish virgin by a depraved maker of images; such seemed Leonora.*"

McCarthy reaches out for one of the three bottles.

"*Such seemed Leonora!*" repeats Franck, before continuing. "*Her complexion, of a dazzling olive hue, was vernal, without any hint of red, not even on the knees or the elbows; the pallor of her slender arms extended into her hands, and of her sloping shoulders into her long neck.*"

The sheriff, with some difficulty, pulls the bottle to him. His eyes shine.

"*She was delicately slender, but nothing of her bone structure was visible. On her flat chest the small, finely shaped breasts were cleanly attached, distant and sharp, with no transitional curves.*"

The bottle is empty. His arm drops, letting it roll on the carpet.

"*The line of her waist swelled slightly at the hips, blending into the excessively long legs of an Eve by Lucas van Leyden.*"

The sheriff reaches out again. Aluminum foil. A small bag of powder.

"*Her slender outlines, the delicacy of her joints, the gracile length of her limbs, the predominance of verticals rendered her flesh, already of an unreal hue, immaterial: she might have been taken for one of those female saints stripped for martyrdom by Schongauer's burin.*"

Then he picks up the spoon…

"*But the ambiguous gaze of her green eyes, the disturbing smile on her broad mouth, the old-gold flavescence of her hair, her entire head, refuted the mysticism of her body.*"

…which also drops to the ground.

"*But soon they were embarrassed by their nakedness, and Bianca snuffed out the candelabras.*"

Franck falls silent. The lights come on again. Then he leaps off the bed and comes back to sit opposite McCarthy, who, after a few moments' hesitation, applauds him violently.

"Did you like that?" asks the detective.

"Yes, yes! What a voice you have! A beautiful, magnificent voice! Like an organ, but better, much better than in church…"

"Thank you, Paul."

"No." (He almost falls off his chair.) "It's for me to thank you! To thank you for everything!"

"Not at all! I just invited you to dinner."

"Oh, more than that, let me tell you... You've spoiled me!"

"You've no idea how true that is, Sheriff. But we're not done yet... We still have the night before us. What would you say to a little more dessert?"

"Well, I'd say that's one hell of a good idea! Shake on it!"

He holds out his hand, which Franck doesn't take.

"Pass the powder," he orders. The sheriff slides the envelope across the table.

"Now the spoon, please."

McCarthy bends down, picks it up, and passes it to the detective. Franck puts the cocaine into it. From his pockets he takes an elegantly decorated silver flask, encrusted with tiny sapphires, which is filled with ammonia.

"My Zippo?" he asks the policeman. McCarthy starts, pats his uniform, and finally produces the lighter.

"Thanks."

Franck pours the ammonia into the spoon and brings it level with his eyes, which have an eager, almost obscene glint; then he slowly combines the two substances using the flame of his Zippo. He wipes up the remaining solids using a tissue, and places them on a smooth, straight-edged scrap of foil. The sheriff holds the foil while Franck, again using the flame of his lighter, heats the solid from below. Soon there remains only a small amber drop, which the two men smoke voluptuously.

*

"Getting it up, Sheriff?" Franck briefly inspects his fly. "No… Too bad."

They are stretched out on the bed.

"You see, Paul, this is what I call a party. Now that the word has become a meaningless entry in our dictionary – meaningless because what it represents has taken over our world – I maintain that the only real parties are intimate, private ones. Here we are with our liberty (what's left of it!), just our own selves (what's left of them!); I mean without the organizers, communicators, and event planners who dam rivers and pack down the earth so well that it's become impossible to sink into it, to lose yourself in it – adorable sorceress, do you love the dammed? Ha ha! Freedom Day, World Book Day, Human Rights Day, Poetry Day; processions, carnivals, independence festivities, jingoistic bacchanalia; celebrations of the equinox, pop concerts, Lollapalooza. It's all so impoverished, sad, vulgar, public. It's only in the bedroom that sedition is possible – what am I saying, Sheriff? – in the *suite*… in *our* suite! Government snoops of the world unite! – They're alarmed to the point of risking scandal, defying the electorate, slapping the people in the face. A regime can only survive with a cop in every house. It's only on that condition you can talk about lasting forever. Look at me, Paul, look at me!"

With difficulty, McCarthy turns toward him.

"Wouldn't anyone think I was talking politics? It's rather comical, isn't it? Yes, I'm blathering, I'm jabbering on, talking too much. But what can you do, what you call 'drugs,' 'hard drugs,' 'narcotics,' are a simple – but effective, and delicious – inducer of thoughts. You can feel them welling up in you, your thoughts, can't you? A surge! A tide! Coming together! Yes, coming together! Now we're truly endowed with personality!"

The sheriff remains silent; he is staring at the ceiling, hands trembling.

"As for our party, since a party it is, let me assure you that you *will* remember it! The Greeks had a sense of the spectacular, and the Romans too! But the mood has changed... We've had to beat a retreat, rein in our energy, contain our frenzy behind closed doors. Oh! There were still great processions, splendid festivities, but there was no more... *possession*. Are you possessed, Sheriff? The best way to prevent possession is never to be yourself. Take the leap! Up and away! Far from ourselves! We'll smoke again, I give you my word! But watch out: I've no word to give! Or rather: I have a word, but no mouth. And no mouth because I've no face, you see? No one can wear a mask for very long, says Seneca. But I could only wear a face for even less time. We've gotten to know one another today, and I'm glad of that. What kind of an impression did I make on you? Seriously? Have you actually met Franck? Is Franck this person stretched out beside you, high on coke, plastered with makeup, a porn star cutout? God only knows! Take a look! But all you'll get is a fragment... a speck of dust. A speck like what you've snorted, which stands for Franck but is never all of him. But why should you care? You've got other fish to fry... A whole panful. Your family! What a joke, a splendid trick, this Marshall and his confession! A trick! The real world makes a fool of you, takes you down a peg, Sheriff – but always with a smile. A smile I've lost, because I've no mouth anymore, because I've... I've told you already! I'm repeating myself. The real world repeats itself too, by the way. What about another smoke? You're not answering?"

McCarthy, pale, brings a hand to his heart. "Water!" he croaks. "Give me water, Franck!"

Franck is on his feet in an instant. "Paul! Come on! Paul!" He slaps him twice, lightly, on the face. "Paul! You're turning pale!" The detective rushes to the minibar, takes out a bottle of brandy, and brings the neck to the sheriff's lips. "Drink this, it'll do you good."

McCarthy takes several gulps, and then violently turns his head away.

"You're getting a bit of color back! You're not a red-faced guy, not ruddy like your colleagues in the detective division. You haven't got a Grecian profile, yet you're more finely formed than your basic Yank. I'll take this opportunity to tell you that among all the arts, sculpture is the one that leaves me coldest. Now why is that? Maybe it's because, unlike painting or literature, it obliges me to go somewhere, to appreciate it from the middle of a crowd, in a museum. Art loses its power when it's prostituted to the herd. Like partying, like the individual, like anything great. The pack hungers for dead meat; it turns everything into Culture. Producing Culture means making nothingness sing, whereas a reproduction of a painting, or a book, can be appreciated in solitude, in exile, in the illusion of its singularity. I was talking about jokes. Your family, Paul. Your neighborhood. Your equilibrium. Yet here you are, this evening, on the verge of fainting, as high as a kite, stretched out alongside a killer... Yes!

Yes, Paul!" He raises his voice. "Look at me!" McCarthy, still pale, looks at Franck. "I'm a murderer! I've killed someone, Sheriff! Arrest me! I tell you, I'm a murderer! And a lot of other things besides... You're a cop and a father. But me... I've got more strings to my bow, more than one card up my sleeve! I try to deceive the real world. But you're its accomplice. You went along with the farce quite consciously. You should have gone mad, but you became colorless. Your kingdom is well worth a heart attack! Poor guy! Stretched out beside Franck, the Francks, you remind me of that hag in the Ensor painting, mercilessly surrounded by masks. Aren't you going to drink this brandy? Drink, I tell you! Hey!" He brings the bottle to McCarthy's lips. "Do you know what tonight reminds me of? I had a young girl of about fourteen stretched out on my bed, blonde, naked. I went down on her, tasted her. Her smell: light, almost a breeze. Her eyes remote, her eyelids heavy with drugs and eyeshadow, she was almost comatose. It was then I knew love. For a few seconds. Aren't you my pupil this evening? My languorous little blonde?" He draws closer to the sheriff. "Do you think you're able to resist me? No, my dear friend. You can't anymore. It's too late! All your life you've resisted. Your crazy, drunken parents that you've tried to forget, to bury beneath your impeccable garden. The house of the dead, like a citadel that you've constructed. Your career, your family, your activities in the community. And along I come. Along comes Marshall. Old Jimmy's ghost. Reality comes back in a flood: all that's left is for you to drown. What? You're turning pale! Yet my coke was almost pure. Like that little blonde girl. Did I tell you about purity? My ideal? 'Ideal' is a big word. Anyway, for someone who has lost the sense of reality, words are all too big, too vague. They no longer work as signs, but like formulas, like mantras that you repeat to avoid finding yourself drained dry, robbed of speech, to help maintain the illusion that you have something to say. Anyway, it was because of a word – a play on words – that poor Lyllian died. You see, we were about to become friends, and I wanted to snort some coke, and it occurred to me that I could make a pun by saying, 'I'm drawing a line under our friendship.' I needed a drug, and I got it! A dead friend, and I got one! You know as well as I do that people will kill for a cigarette, for a scrape, for an insult. I killed for a pun. The whole thing is dizzyingly, frighteningly lacking in substance. It's nothing; that's what scares you. What can you do? All you know is the farce, and I know nothing but impulse. What about a little more?"

"No, no, please—"

"Come on, Sheriff, you've got your color back. And even so, your pallor makes you more seductive. Has no one ever told you that?"

No answer.

Irritated, Franck raises his voice. "I'm talking to you, Sheriff! I'm asking you if you know how to dance!"

He grabs McCarthy's hands and forces him to his feet. Then he starts the Fauré "Elegy" on the CD player. "Sheriff, let's dance!" he exclaims. "Let's dance! Dance till we go nuts, till we shatter, pulverize ourselves! Let's get pulverized, you old devil! Sheriff! I'll teach you… Follow me! Follow me far away! Ready! Keep following me! Hey! I'm talking to you! Start moving! Let's dance! Let's dance!"

The suite is dark again. The scent of Casablanca lilies has replaced the smell of ammonia. A window is open. Sitting on either side of the table, with a bottle of cognac – an excellent Martell Cordon Bleu – between them, the two men are facing one another. Franck has removed his makeup and gotten fully dressed; his eyes are mournful.

"You're a free man," declares the sheriff, gravely.

Franck refills McCarthy's glass before answering, "You're mistaken. I offered you a feast, drugs, we danced. I introduced you to Péladan. From that you've concluded that I'm an original…" He sighs. "But it's quite the opposite. What we had this evening – which I had the cheek to call a 'party' – was basically just a series of everyday clown's tricks, judiciously strung along the tightrope of necessity. And you'll see the result! You'll vomit once or twice, your heart will beat fast, you'll suffer a bit from withdrawal, your life will resume its flow, and you'll drown in it. As for mine, it has been hit hard. Maybe compromised… I'm dislocated, lost – there are killers on my trail." He gets up and takes the suitcase he has packed. In the doorway, he turns around.

"I'm very glad to have gotten to know you, Sheriff. Try to vacate the room before eleven." He goes out.

Franck crosses the underground garage whistling Interpol's "Slow Hands." He keeps a hand in his pocket, a finger on the trigger. A look around reassures him that all is quiet: no one, empty cars. He arranges his things in the passenger compartment of the 300C, connects his GPS, takes out a cigarette, lights it, and, reflecting that he has made some splendid encounters, admired several masterpieces, killed a man, and made a few amusing puns, he drives away.